A ROYAL ISSUE

And Other Fateful Tales

John Margeryson Lord

Order this book online at www.trafford.com
or email orders@trafford.com

Most Trafford titles are also available at major online book retailers.

Printed in the United States of America.

ISBN: 978-1-4907-2521-5 (sc)
ISBN: 978-1-4907-2522-2 (e)

Library of Congress Control Number: 2014901288

Trafford rev. 01/22/2014

 www.trafford.com
North America & international
toll-free: 1 888 232 4444 (USA & Canada)
fax: 812 355 4082

?**?**??

DEDICATION

This small collection of Short Stories is dedicated to my brother David Nicholson—Lord whose book entitled THE DOWNRISING The Coming Apocalypse* has recently been released. The plot follows a series of loosely connected events which take place following the breakdown of our fragile social and political structures.

The book is well written, David being a much more prescient writer than me.

I wish the book great success.

?? ??

CONTENTS

Dedication v

* What Was It About Him?................................... 1

* The Smoking Chimney.. 9

* Wealth 23

* What Price Riches? 31

* The Luckiest Man on the Planet....................... 37

* The Zoo 47

* The Girl In Question... 57

* Of Golden Hair 75

* Stick... 85

* The Whereabouts 93

* A Royal Issue 113

* Murder—The Only Way................................. 125

WHAT WAS IT ABOUT HIM?

*I*t had been a very, very long two years. He had been taken from her at the peak of their relationship. She had needed every day of those twenty-four long months to get used to the idea that he was never coming back. Never again would she hear that cheery voice following the front door being thrust open to be followed by his sure footfall. His greeting was never the same two days running.

'Hi toots, your favourite man has arrived.'

Or again—

'Prepare yourself Joy has arrived at this house.'

Or simply—

'What's for tea I'm desperate.'

He liked to surprise her, and mostly he succeeded.

Quite often he would enter carrying a bunch of flowers or when in that special mood a small gift usually of a sexy implication, which would indicate an early night.

He was a good deal older than she but was vigorous enough to keep her contented.

Any problem and he would smile at her with those lovely brown-green eyes and her heart would melt.

He had been taken from her in a most cruel manner. They had no warning. He had spent the best part of the morning gardening, an activity that he very much enjoyed, Having cleaned himself up he sat with the newspaper to finish the crossword. When she went to tell him that lunch was ready she found him dead.

A sudden massive heart attack they said.

Of course she missed him, but she was still young and attractive with strong physical desires.

Now, here she was. Much later on a coach trip to a nearby city. She recalled seeing the day out advertised in the local library and decide to treat herself. Later remembering, a thrill ran down her spine, as for the umpteenth time she went over that wonderful feeling that took her by surprise, the one that she thought she would never experience again. It was then that she first saw him and felt the strange inner certainty that he would come to mean everything to her.

The day of the trip was sunny and rich with promise. She was on the last minute for the coach and as she climbed aboard she saw that all the seats were taken—except one.

He stood as she approached and grinning suggestively offered her the window seat. She thanked him and sat.

His starting ploy was conventional enough.

'Have you been to York before?' He asked politely.

'No. Have you?' She asked.

'Yes I have, and I can tell you that you are in for treat. It has everything—old worldly shops and eating places. Lots of fascinating historical sites to look at. And,—Some pubs of great character.'

'Sounds interesting.' She said.

Then he made his move.

'Perhaps you might let me show you around?' He asked hesitantly. 'I would be delighted.'

All very conventional—so why was her heart beating so violently?

'That would be very nice, thank you.' She acknowledged.

'No,' he said gallantly, 'thank you—the pleasure will be mine.'

And so it began.

He bought two tickets for the Yorvic train which took you on an historical journey based on York, After which they had a delightful lunch in an old worldly pub down by the river. Marks on the wooden beams supporting the ceiling indicated the water level at times when a swollen river had invaded the place. When that happened, as it had many times before, they simply moved upstairs the landlord told them.

Vick, as he was called, was an entertaining companion with a ready wit and a heart melting smile, and the time passed too quickly. They were just able to do a little shopping before making a dash for the returning coach. He even bought her a small handbag she had admired, 'As a memento of the visit.' He said.

They were both quite tired on the return trip and discussion was at its minimal allowing her to take advantage of the window seat and enjoy the countryside they were passing through.

It was at journey's end that things suddenly took a step forward as it were.

As they left the coach Vick waved a cab over and asked her if he could give her a lift. It was now growing dark and this was the part of the day that she was not looking forward to. 'Yes please, it is not far,' she said.

'Good. Where to then?' He asked.

She gave the taxi man her address and they climbed aboard.

'I hope This isn't taking you out of your way.' She told him.

'No it's fine,' he replied.

'It's only a couple of minutes walk, and it is a nice night for a stroll.'

As the taxi drew away and left them standing by her gate, she wondered what he would do. To her surprise she felt her heart beating strongly. Then unexpectedly she found that she did not want him to leave. She was enjoying his company and wanted it to continue.

'We have only just met.' She said to herself. 'I need to be careful.' But she need not have worried.

'Well then—its Good Night, And I hope to see you again very soon. I must say your company made the trip for me. Er . . . . could I take you for lunch or even dinner sometime in the near future—say tomorrow?' He asked hesitantly. And in the exchange that followed, a dinner date was arranged for a couple of days hence.

Tired as she was, she watched him until he had vanished round the corner. He gave her a little wave as he disappeared.

She did not sleep well.

Her thoughts chased each other round and round. Would he come to mean anything to her, Was she ready or was it too soon. Did he like her. She would have to book a hair appointment before the date. She wanted to look her best.

Should she invite him in. What if he wanted to stay the night—it had been such a long time. If he did—could she respond or would the image of her dead husband get in the way. What would the neighbours think—or did she care.

She wondered just what he was really like, it had been a long day and trouble free. What was he like in an emergency?

What was his job? And even—was he already married?

Questions, questions, and still more questions and no answers.

As sleep eventually took over she pictured his face, a pleasant even attractive one, but what was it that was special—her very last thought was of his brilliant smiling eyes. Eyes that were full of laughter, and the joy of living.

The time seemed to pass very quickly in spite of her anxiety, and in due course the date they had agreed arrived. She was so nervous that she actually considered cancelling their meeting—but she had no idea how to contact him.

What to wear? She did not know where they might dine. Casual or semi formal? She had no way of guessing—in the end she chose a simple evening dress that was flattering but not too severe. Blue to match her eyes.

Eyes !!! That was what was troubling her, what was it about his eyes?

Her door chime startled her at spot on the agreed time.

A last glance in the mirror, and satisfied by what she saw, she tugged the heavy door which did its usual trick of catching on the carpet, and it took a good shove from the other side to cause it to swing open.

And there he stood smiling at her.

It seemed a long time before either of them spoke.

5

'Gosh! But don't you look nice. The taxi's waiting, shall we go?'

He took her arm as she stepped out closing the door with a good tug behind her.

'Do you like Italian food?' he asked as the taxi moved off.

She felt a flood of relief.

'I love it.' She said smiling at him.

'Good,' he said, 'I thought that you might. Do you know Marko's in Mason Street?'

She said that she had not been there, but had often wondered what it was like.

'Well you are about to find out, I think you will approve—Marko is a friend of mine—known each other for years.'

Marko himself welcomed them and saw that they were comfortably seated as he waved the wine waiter over to take their order.

Her attention was everywhere, and the food was proper Italian and not the usual English imitation and very beautifully served.

It struck her that they made a very handsome couple as she became aware of the many admiring glances from the other diners. Marko made a fuss of them and she revelled in the atmosphere.

It was as they were sipping the last of the wine that it popped into her thoughts unasked, just as it had before.

—What exactly was it about his eyes? She reached into her mind for an answer—but the knowledge would not surface.

But his eyes said it all—that he was enjoying himself just as much as she. She could not remember afterwards what they talked about, but the conversation never flagged. He did not say much about himself although she did learn that he had a well paid job, was single and lived on his own. But whether or not he had been married or engaged she was non the wiser. If she enquired of him he would skilfully turn it round to her likes and dislikes.

One thing was clear to them both—that mostly they took great pleasure in much the same things.

In other words—"they got on." as they say.

But what was it with those eyes?

The evening so far was agreed by both parties to have been a very enjoyable success.

Taxi home and he took her hand and held it as she alighted.

What now? She wondered, her heart racing.

At her door—'May I kiss you?' He asked.

And he did.

He refused her offer to come in for a last drink with the excuse of an early start the next day. 'Next time.' He said.

She had a very disturbed night and at breakfast the next day realised that she wanted him in every sense of the phrase.

But those beautiful eyes—what the heck was it?

It was still niggling away at the back of her mind.

He phoned and they dated again—this time she had prepared a meal which he clearly enjoyed and afterwards he admired her home making.

It was mutual. And seemed to be natural—they made love on her settee.

And it was good—and they knew there would be more.

So over the following months they saw much of each other. He cooked her a meal at his flat where she stayed the night. She noted that he was tidy but not un-naturally so.

It soon became obvious that the relationship was getting serious, and it began to puzzle her that whereas he had told her about his past relationships he had shown no curiosity about hers. He had not once asked her about her late husband.

But she found that it did not matter to her at all.

Then one evening as they were relaxing after making love she happened to mention her husband by his Christian name—Osborn.

He sat up with a startled expression—'Did you say he was called Osborn? He asked.

'Tell me—what was his surname?'

'Morrison.' She said simply.

'Why?'

He was lost in thought for some time.

'Did you know him?' She asked.

He regarded her with a strange expression.

'He was my father.' He said. 'He left us when I was young.'

***

Then it came to her—those eyes—those hauntingly lovely brown-green eyes of course—they were his—her husband's—and his father's

JML
2/3/2013

THE SMOKING CHIMNEY

*T*hat was the whole trouble with older properties—there was always something that required fixing. If it wasn't the heating it was a misbehaving electrical plug or a door knob that came away in one's hand.

Still it was her own choice, Susan had dreamed of living there since childhood. 'Don't be silly dear—it would be far beyond your means.' her loving parent would insist.

But she could dream.

And when the seriously wealthy Lloyds bought the place she recognised the possibilities when she saw their youngest lad, Lance. Almost the same age as herself and a keen athlete she laid plans to get to know him, and to her surprise she found that she liked him, liked him very much indeed.

Then the old man took ill and was advised to live in a warmer climate and the family moved to the Mediterranean leaving young Lance to finish his schooling back home, as a lodger in her house.

What followed was almost inevitable.

Lance got her pregnant—or so it was thought and the family returned for the wedding. But the baby proved to be just a bad bout of wind., and the old ones couldn't wait to get back to the sun. The old house was something of a financial embarrassment but both she and Lance loved the place in which he had never lived, but which held many happy memories for them both. It was the utter peace of the place that they liked. They both revelled in the quiet when all that disturbed the tranquillity was the chirping and calling of the wide variety of birds that regularly visited the large garden.

And so the day arrived when Lance landed a good job as Clerk of Parks for the Council and our recently married couple moved into the big house. As the place had not been lived in for some time there was a great deal to do just to make a small part of it habitable. It was summer and a seriously hot one, and they were able to go through the place chucking out all the old stuff that was beyond the end of its life. They were in no hurry and decided that it would take as long as it took to furnish the house to their own taste—and that they would do so at their own pace—one room at a time—starting with the lounge.

Mostly an inconvenient place to run. It nevertheless had a nice airy feel about it, with a sizable kitchen and a comfortable lounge, where sat the large TV purchased by the grace of Lance's first wage packet.

This lounge was heated by an enormous log fire which sat under a rather grand stone canopy.

On each side of the fire was an ingle-nook stone seat almost completely under the canopy.

The big disadvantage of this arrangement was that be nice and warm seated by the fire, or you could sit in the settee and watch TV, but to do both was difficult.

But they were happy.

Lance promised to find a way round the problem.
It all seemed a bit too easy—
And it was.

***

Nothing untoward happened in the first couple of months as they settled in. The summer was sunny and hot and most of their free time was spent outside attending to the flower beds or mowing the extensive lawns. Or simply lazing in the easy deckchairs which they found in the garden shed. They had no need to use up any of the stack of logs laid up for the winter months by Sam the elderly gardener and odd job man.

Two resident families nearby and worked in the big house in exchange for their cottage accommodation. Sam and his family occupied one of these comfortable places,

And their cleaner Maisie and her lot the other.

Sam and Maisie had always been regarded as part of the estate, a situation happily continued by Lance and Susan.

They had just about settled in at the end of the first six months or so, and to date,

Lance with Sam's assistance had dealt easily with any problems that had arisen. And they had done so without the need for outside help.

It was as they felt that they had got most of the place under some sort of control, that they were faced with a situation so serious that they were tempted to leave this place that they loved so much.

The effect at times was as if they were living in a waking nightmare. Their dreams of solitude gone.

It all began quite suddenly and without any warning in that comfortable lounge one quiet and to begin with—uneventful summer's evening.

Susan was watching a soap on TV and Lance was sitting in an ingle nook concentrating on the newspaper's version of the local football derby.

Outside there was a fairly gentle breeze blowing from the north-west as it had done from their first day.

Now however a sudden change took the wind round to the south-east and it began to gust quite strongly.

In the lounge they heard it before they saw it.

There was a kind of moan followed by a loud 'woosh'. And then a cloud of black smoke billowed out from under the canopy and into the room where it swirled round covering everything with a layer of fine grey dust, and set the pair of them coughing.

They did not wait, with watering eyes they quickly made for the door.

Once outside and with the door shut they looked at each other and would have laughed if it had not been so shocking—they resembled a pair of crows with just their eyes peering out of faces covered in grey dust.

As they coughed and spluttered they found it difficult to see as the grit found its way into their eyes from which tears made pink rivers down their cheeks.

Lance was the worst having been directly in the path of the soot fall.

'Bl**dy Hell!' He exclaimed through bouts of coughing. 'What in heaven's name caused that?'

Just then a second icy blast swept under the closed door and chased along the corridor leaving a mess of thick sooty dust.

'What do we do now?' Asked Susan, without expecting a reply. 'I'm not going back in there tonight.'

So they each took a shower and settled for an early night and a good read.

What else they did is not recorded.

***

By dawn the following morning the wind had all but ceased and a bright yellow sun had begun to warm the day.

When Susan found the courage to open the lounge door and peered in, she wanted to cry. Everything, absolutely everything was covered with a dirty gritty layer of black soot. Nothing had escaped its attention—TV, sideboard, chairs, carpets, absolutely everything, even the flowers in the vase on the table.

Breakfast was a council of war.

Lance voiced the view that there must be a partial blockage in the chimney resulting in a build up of soot, when a sudden change of wind direction dislodged it and blew it downwards.

'What do we do?' Wailed Susan.

Lance considered the problem.

'Firstly we must prevent any more soot entering the lounge. I will get Sam to help me with that.' He paused for thought.

'After the room has been quarantined, we should do our best to clean the place up. Then we should get the chimney swept by a qualified chimney-sweep. I bet Sam will know someone.'

And so the first phase of the chimney war began.

And it got worse—much, much worse.

***

It took much effort on everyone's part to get the chimney temporarily sealed and some semblance of order and cleanliness achieved in the lounge. And Sam did know of a good chimney-sweep in the village. Lance checked at the pub and was satisfied that Edward (Ted) Robinson was highly recommended, and was contacted and hired to do the job.

He could not start immediately, he said, for other promised jobs, but could fit them in in two weeks time. And so it was arranged.

It was during this lull in the proceedings that Susan declared that she was unhappy with strange people wandering about the place.

It was the sheer size of the house and its extensive grounds which made it impossible to keep an eye on visitors and workmen. However on the due date Susan opened the door to Ted Robinson who stood there with his bag of brushes.

Lance took himself off to do a job in the garden that badly needed fixing.

In the lounge and with Susan's help Ted spread good clean sheets over the furniture and any exposed areas of carpet.

At this juncture Susan provided them with both with a cup of tea, and Ted began to regale Susan with tales of past adventures of his chimney sweeping.

'It's these very old houses and their big chimneys that can give one a surprise.' He began. 'More than once I have discovered the remains of a hen or other farm bird which has been shoved down the chimney to sweep it clean and had got stuck. It used to be the standard way. Too bad for the bird eh!'

He grinned at Susan's long face.

'And once I found a metal box which contained a whole stack of old faded black and white photographs of men and women doing very unusual sexual things to each other.'

He heaved a great sigh. 'No one owned up to having put it there, but the owner looked somewhat embarrassed,'

And with that he screwed the brush onto the end of the first rod, and inserted it up the wide chimney breast. As he added more rods soot came down by the bucket-full.

Suddenly Ted tugged hard on the rods.

'What the Hell!,' he muttered. 'They seem to be stuck.'

He struggled with the rods for some time, with no success.

'I'm afraid I shall have to climb up inside the fireplace and try and see what is holding the damn thing, it's probably a loose brick or something. But I shall need a light of some sort.'

Susan went and quickly returned with Lance's big all purpose torch.

Ted pulled the sheets to one side and climbed in under the canopy. All she could see of him was his feet.

He pulled and pushed for some time with no success.

Then suddenly 'What the Hell!'

Ted re-appeared from under the sheet looking extremely dirty and dishevelled and clutching in his hands several bones.

When he got clear, he looked down at his find and echoed her own thoughts. 'I do hope that they don't prove to be human or we'll have the police crawling all over the place and asking daft questions.

'I'll leave the sheets where they are—my rods are still stuck. And I'll take these bones to the vets—he'll know if they belonged to a person.'

***

When told about the bones Lance asked Ted if he could see them, and it only took him a minute or so before he said with a chuckle—

'It's a dog.'

This was confirmed later that day. '—A boxer if I'm not mistaken.' He added.

Later Susan and Lance were enjoying an evening glass of wine, and naturally the conversation was all about the find.

'But what on earth was a dog doing up there ?' Susan persisted in asking.

'I have no idea.' Said Lance. 'But there appears to be a deep square hole built into the brickwork which seems to have something quite big in it—and there are more bones according to Ted. What I too don't understand is what on earth a dog was doing up the chimney? It looks like we will have to wait until tomorrow to find out.'

Ted was early the next day and eager to begin. Leaving his rods and brushes un-used,

He rapidly disappeared up the chimney armed with the big torch and a fair sized hammer.

In the lounge Lance sat ready with a box of tools ready in case they were needed. Susan watched from the door.

For some time all that our two house owners was a knocking interrupted by some colourful swearing from Ted accompanied by regular falls of unpleasant black dust.

Then suddenly to their horror a huge slab of stone fell out of the chimney breast and into the room leaving a gaping hole through which they could see a portion of Sam's startled face.

No one spoke.

They did not know what to say.

'Blimey,' exclaimed Lance 'What do we do now? You had better come down Ted.'

'Just a moment.' Came Ted's voice from the chimney-breast. 'There seems to be something here—I can probably push it out into the room. Can you get a ladder Lance,

And try to get it from your side?'

Lance soon returned with a ladder and between them they wrestled out of the chimney-breast a dirty black metal box about the size of a large shoe box.

He climbed down with the box clutched in his hands and set it down on the cloth covered table. Whilst a grinning Ted emerged from the chimney.

Only Susan laughed. 'Hidden treasure,' she exclaimed. ' Come on then you chaps open it up—can't wait.'

Lance said 'You've got the tool to do the job Ted, so go ahead and lets know the worst.'

It took just two blows on the ancient metal with hammer and chisel and the box burst open.

For a while no one spoke.

What they saw was truly unbelievable.

There lying snugly on a red cushion, and glinting with a bright gold colour was a bust, with its face grinning up at them as it lay.

They looked and still could not believe it.

It was finally put into words by Ted who whispered almost to himself—

'It's the devil—a gold bust of Satan.'

Lance was about to reach over and take it from its box but as prevented from doing so by Susan.

'Please don't. It's EVIL—just look at that grin.'

They were all affected—the thing as a sculpture's masterpiece, one could feel the hatred and the vile intentions displayed on that truly frightening face.

***

They tried to keep it to themselves, but this was not possible in such a close village, and it was only a matter of time before the press got onto it, and a fierce debate started as to where the bust came from and how and why it came to be in the chimney and in their house?

And the dog—what was it doing there? They became determined to find out. Several experts were consulted who declared it to be old and cast in real gold. But if they truly knew the answers they were keeping them to themselves

But a couple became to be more communicative and told something of the history of the thing.

Round about the early seventeen hundreds the bust was created and worshipped by a very strange sect who revered the Devil and all his works. The house was their meeting place, and it was from there that their evil work was planned and carried out.

They were suspected of terrible mal-practice and were eventually sent packing. It was said that the dog was originally chained to the wall in the hollowed out place to act as guard.

In the Tate gallery was found an old painting of the interior of the house as it was then. The bust had pride of place in front of a roaring fire in the fireplace. The artist was unknown, the style being unique.

The thing itself was found to be made of pure gold worth a considerable fortune. But in spite of this Susan declared that she would have nothing to do with any gain from its sale.

***

At first Susan and Lance enjoyed the situation in which they were key witnesses to the find.

They were often on TV, and being interviewed by the press. But they soon found that were having to fend off impertinent questions—like 'How did you now it was there ?'

'Is that why you bought the house?' and 'How long have you been devil worshipers?

And worse.

In the village they began to be suspected as being behind any adverse happenings. There were always people happy to blame someone for the occasional accident or misfortune.

They had phone calls and letters from all over the world as the international press got to know.

But when some representatives from strange sects started to arrive demanding to see and even touch the object, Susan expressed her frustration at having no time to themselves anymore. And it was getting worse.

Their privacy had been breached and there seemed always to be some-one trying to find out more.

There was nothing that they could do to escape. And so, after a serious discussions as to what to do, a few things were decided.

It was not just getting rid of the thing—there were plenty of offers for it. And the house itself was a massive attraction.

They made up their minds to move.

But before they could, the future was decided or them.

They chose to have a holiday first. Two weeks away from it all would see them renewed. And in the meantime they had got Ted with some help from Sam to replace the bust where it had been all those years and to repair the chimney-breast to as near as possible as to how it had been when they found it. Then they packed and left for a small island off the coast of Italy for two weeks of sun and relaxation.

It was on their return that they had another shock. Sam who was supposed to be keeping an eye on the house whilst they were away, was taken ill with an undefined complaint leaving the place un-guarded.

On their return our pair found the house the same as when they left it but on entering the lounge they discovered that the chimney breast had been breached and the artefact gone. Strangely there were signs of great heat surrounding the hole.

All investigations drew a blank.

The thing was never seen again. The couple moved out. The public lost interest. The house having lost its attraction, remained empty, and gradually mouldered into the ground.

Sam made a complete and rapid recovery.

John Lord
10/3/2013

WEALTH

*T*hey were born in the same street in the year that heralded the end of World War Two. But there the similarity ended. Sarah Broen's father had somehow missed the call-up to join one of the services and had continued to run his late father's engineering factory. Situated on the outskirts of one of our larger cities the place had missed the bombing and had not lost a single day's work throughout the conflict.

In fact they had won a singular honour in being presented with a medal for their dedication—they worked throughout all the local air-raids and had put in a record number of overtime hours of continuous output. This ensured that at the end of hostilities the business had made an awful lot of money. The Old Man, as he was known, considered that the business would continue to make him quite wealthy.

His daughter Sarah had money to burn. Happiest when out shopping she would spend a small fortune on a dress that she had seen confident in the knowledge that there was plenty more where that came from. Even though there was not a great deal of choice since rationing continues for some time after peace was declared. And she always went for the most expensive. But it has to be said that she always looked elegant.

She was one of those lucky people who could look good in almost anything and was a sophisticated model for everything that she wore.

The street was about equally divided between those who despised her, reckoning that she betrayed her class, and those who simply envied her and would willingly change places.

Sarah even had her own income, rare for someone who was only fifteen. She was paid good money for a trivial job in the factory office, where she did menial jobs when she bothered to turn up, such as brewing up and emptying the waste paper baskets, or sorting the post.

Two things prevented her from being disliked. She was a 'looker' having near perfect features and figure, which she had inherited from her attractive mother; and she was charming and modestly friendly. Her kind nature meant that she was always ready to help anyone who asked for her support.

If you knew anyone who lived in the street you would know Sarah.

***

The far end of the street was the 'poor' end, overshadowed by the towering brick arches which carried the railway on its way to the city. Stacked closely there were several rows of terraced dwellings.

These were mostly 'two-up and two down' just big enough to bring up a small family. The sun never reached here even at the height of summer.

Tom Spencer's father owned no factory when he took a German bullet in the chest.

It killed him just as it was designed to do.

Tom found that he had to find some way of supporting his younger brother and his mother on the meagre income that a thankful government presented them with each week. He left school with no useful qualifications and took the only job that no-one else wanted. He was what you might call a 'bin man' removing other people's rubbish. The family were however 'happy' as judged by the standards of the poor end of the road. After all they lived in an environment they understood with few pressures and lots of free time to meet and chat with the other inhabitants of the street. And the war was over at last.

But Arthur Spencer never came back.

Life seemed to be unchanging. The daily round was only relieved by a visit, if one was flush, to the public house at the end of the street. To live here a man was expected to support one or other of the cities football teams, the Greens or the Blacks as they were locally known. Rivalry was fierce and took up most of the conversation at the public bar, Tom had reached the age at which he was allowed to stand at the bar and order a gill. No-one got drunk—they couldn't afford to.

It was about then on one of those dreary Friday evenings that Tom having hitherto had nothing to do with girls happened on Sarah. I say happened on, but it was more of a head-on kind of thing. Both turned the same corner from opposite directions. Sarah's carrier bag was not man enough to withstand the unexpected bump it received, its contents spilling out onto the pavement.

Tom full of apologies bent to pick up the scattered items, and it was when he looked up that it happened.

He had never seen anything quite so beautiful, so perfect, so heart racing, as she smiled down on him.

From then on he could think of nothing else

It did not even need him to be near her—he simply drowned in the knowledge of her.

He could no longer remember a time when he did not know her. It created a longing that came to mean everything in his young life.

It was as if she were already part of him. His feelings were both joyful and extremely painful.

Hard working lad that he was, his friends often had to scold him to break the reverie that he was apt to fall into.

And the whole street knew.

Half despised him as they considered he was wasting his time mooning over someone who was well above him in wealth and prospects.

Whilst the other half thought that as a good looking lad—they would make a grand couple and wished them well.

Poor old Tom, he had no money to take her out, and wouldn't know where to take her if he had. Nothing to buy her a small gift or flowers or any little thing that she may have set her heart on. All he could do was to look with a painful longing.

His mother tried to get him to recognise that his ambitions towards Sarah were hopeless and that he should forget her. But how on earth could he do that, with them both living in the same street?

Tom's chances stood less than a snowball in Hell!

He even began to loose weight.

And things began to get serious.

Sarah had noticed Tom and liked what she saw. But her mother schooled here-about Tom's lack of wealth and lack of prospects, and Sarah listened.

Tom did his level best.

He saved what he could from his meagre income, just enough to buy her some flowers for her birthday.

A gift that seemed pathetic in view of what her current boyfriend had splashed out on her.

Tom's mother was naturally worried about her son and tried her best to make him see sense and forget Sarah.

'What about Jane Thoms—she would make you a grand wife, more your equal and she is not at all bad looking.' And he would find that she had invited Jane over to share their evening meal—such as it was.

Jane would have settled with Tom, if he had had only given her half a chance.

Sarah and her mother could afford holidays abroad which were just coming into fashion. They went missing from the street for two weeks—a welcome break from the dull routine, Sarah's mother called it. In fact she was determined that her offspring should have every chance to see how the wealthier folk in society set out to enjoy themselves.

Tom was physically sick at the thought of what Sarah might be experiencing, his mind building heart wrenching scenes of Sarah enjoying erotic pleasures long into the night.

He knew that his ambitions towards Sarah were hopeless, but that knowledge did not help in the slightest.

It was towards the end of that bleak two weeks that Tom had an idea. It was simple enough—

HE WOULD GET RICH

Why, he wondered had it not occurred to him before.

But then his heart sank as he realised that—he had no idea whatsoever as to how to set about achieving it.

He had to start somewhere—so he joined the local library, at least it was free. He began to read everything that might help him achieve his ambition. The biographies of the rich and powerful were first on the list.

He put long hours into studying other jobs that would bring in a decent income.

He was so occupied with his studies that he saw little of Sarah on their return from Spain.

He did not notice that she was growing up. Her escorts were now men not boys, and she was looking for a husband not a casual lover. Some were after her relative wealth, others saw her as a wage packet and a very attractive one.

But then nothing stays the same for long.

**

At the end of hostilities that had gripped the world Sarah's father's business was doing very well—

But here's the rub—in peacetime who wants bullets for guns that are no longer in use? Who wants guns designed to fit tanks that were now rapidly becoming out of date. As the owner he soon found that the big military business was now out of his league.

He was competing against those who had friends in high places—men who took back-handers to guarantee that the sweetest contracts came their way—had none.

As orders gradually dried up he began to lay off members of the work force. A workforce that had worked miracles for him during the war. So after a year long struggle against increasing odds and loosing money, he gave in and put the works on the market.

Sarah had to face the fact that her family was now BROKE.

Meanwhile Tom had discovered engineering.

He was still determined to get Sarah but only if he could make enough for them to live as she was used to.

Word of the companies problems circulated at the Hare and Hounds where the sympathies were entirely with the workforce.

One inclement day Tom was looking at pictures of large motorised machines for colleting rubbish and cleaning away the unusable stuff of war.

His enquiries led to his putting together a business plan. He thought of the factory going cheap and all those military vehicles with nowhere to go, And he thought of all those city and township requirements for removing waste. He was now able to communicate with his bank manager and obtain his backing to purchase the works. He concentrated on designing custom built machines to any specification to meet any specialised need of the customer. The more complex the requirement the higher the cost, the greater the profit. He secured some splendid orders. He also had a dedicated work force who would support anyone who could give them jobs.

The vehicles rolled out and the money rolled in.

TOM WAS RICH

So what about Sarah?

What do you think?

Did they marry, have a family, and live happily ever after?

Did he despise Sarah for her hitherto mercenary attitude and marry someone else?

Did he fall for his father's secretary and move in with her?

Did he remain single for the rest of his life?

In fact he did none of these things!

Instead—Tom took an interest in fast cars and raced his Ferrari all over the world. Aged just thirty years old he was killed when he came off the road in practice and in bad weather—leaving Sarah still single and pregnant with his son. His mother sold the firm and moved out of the street into a better house in a village in the country where she lives with Sarah and her grandson.

John Lord
18/3/2013

WHAT PRICE RICHES?

*H*e was taking a short cut through the park. At his age he needed all the short cuts he could find. Tiredness was overtaking him. He had suffered this all embracing weakness more frequently of late.

A bench seat provided a welcome place to recover and he sank gratefully down and drew a deep breath. He was feeling better already.

The day was warm even for early summer, and everywhere there were signs of recovery from a harsh winter.

The oaks were just coming into leaf in an attempt to catch up with the ash trees.

The spaces between them were a vivid green with new grass, and here and there those vivid splashes of colour were the early flowers just bursting into bloom.

Across the path in front of the seat, the dark grey placid surface of the ornamental lake was broken by ducks lazily swimming and resplendent in their brand new summer plumage.

There was hardly a breath of wind, and only the occasional movement of a duck produced bright interlocking circles of ripples which cris-crossed each other as they expanded occasionally flashing with the sun's reflected light. The quiet was stabbed by a solitary wren loudly piping its complex song from a nearby bush whose buds were just about to add their colour to the scene. Here and there were the shiny round tops of fungi tempted out by the warmth of mid-day.

It was about mid-day and he had left his place of work to the surprise of the staff who saw him go. It was usually his practice to call in his secretary and dictate a number of urgently required letters whilst consuming his canteen provided lunch. But on this occasion he had simply risen from his large executive desk and without a word of explanation walked along the corridor and out of the building.

Harold Meeks, a creature of fixed habits, was breaking with routine. It was unique, and he had no idea where he was headed. However chance guided his footsteps and he soon found himself entering the local public park.

He was un-used to physical exercise and after some distance found himself somewhat out breath. As luck would have it he was approaching a park bench which on reaching he sat gratefully to rest himself.

As he relaxed and looked around him, he was struck by the number of flowers that were bursting through the grass around his feet nodding gently to each other. It seemed to him that he had never seen anything quite so vitally alive.

In the quiet of the place he dozed gently for a short while.

It was THEN THAT IT HAPPENED.

As he looked at a group of bright daisies at his feet THEY SPOKE.

Shocked he opened his eyes wide and checked that he was awake and not dreaming.

'Yes it is us that you can hear, but don't worry no-one else can hear us.' Said the daisies.

Feeling rather foolish and looking round to ensure that they could not be overheard, he said—

'This is silly, flowers can't talk. Anyway what do you want with me?'

'Well we have never seen you here before and wonder what bought you here today. You could have done this many times in your life but what was it that was so urgent as to prevent it we wonder?

Are you so busy? Is your business so important?'

This is ridiculous, he thought. It can't be happening—but the implication behind the remark stung him.

'Yes, I would say that what I have accomplished has been due to hard work which has left no time to do this kind of thing.' He said—TO THE DAISY!

'So what then are these accomplishments that occupied you so very much? Do you think that your life has been successful?'

This came from a lone daffodil nodding near his foot.

Again he was stung to reply—

'Well I have succeeded in creating great wealth for my family and in doing so have also made many others quite well off. We don't want for any of life's essentials.'

Of course he was successful his assets added up to a huge fortune. He counted his wealth in millions not mere thousands. His businesses reached right around the globe involving some fifteen countries and many thousands of workers were dependent on his succeeding. If this was not a success just what was.

'I think you will find that I control the destinies of companies and of people all round the world.' He said.

Just then a woman pushing a pram approached and the daisies were silent until she was past.

'All of which is true,' began the daisy, when she had gone. *'But would your wife agree that your marriage has been a success?'*

'Well she has always had everything she said that she wanted—everything.' He said angrily. He did not like the way that this was going. Why should they be attacking him like this? Why did he come here in the first place. He was tempted to stamp on the daisy which was asking these searching questions.

'I wouldn't do that if I were you—there are many more of us than of you, besides you tell us that you have been successful in your life. So why the anger?'

And would your wife agree that she had everything that she wanted as you claim?'

Strangely he felt that he had to tell it as he saw it.

'Of course she did—big house, nice car, super holidays, women to do the housework, a gardener, servants when required, the best clothes money could buy, plenty of pocket money—what more could she want?' He asked.

'But what about affection, tenderness, understanding, loving, sharing, even companionship—what about these riches? Did you give her these?'

For some reason talking to a flower prevented him from pretending but he felt the need to defend himself.

'But she never told me that she wanted these things, in any case providing what I did allowed no time for them.'

'But don't you see—like other people she expected them to come from you—even your secretary sent her flowers on your anniversaries—she claimed that you always said you were too busy to bother. And by the way you treated her the just the same.' This from a small group of crocuses nodding nearby.

'So you are all ganging up on me are you?'

'No we are just telling you as it is. Your life is not the success you think it is.' Spoke a lone wood anemone by his foot.

'And what about your son and your daughter? Did they wallow in your affection? No you were only too happy to see them off the premises having made it very clear that since you had made the grade—it then it was up to them to do the same. You are fortunate that it all turned out as well as it did. But you should have gone to Laurence's wedding and Susan's daughter's christening.'

He wondered vaguely how they knew these things.

'There was too much money at stake—I just couldn't make it. Is that so wrong? After all I bought Laurence a new car to make up for it. Isn't that enough?'

There was a chorus of No's.

The last words were left to the daisies.

'We are sorry that you still think that your life has been a success, but we would beg to differ. Tenderness, understanding, kindness, love, thoughtfulness, generosity (other than monetary), and consideration, and just plain interestedness.

These and other things like them were all missing. Many friends as well as your family would like to have got closer to you but you discouraged it.

'No, measured against these qualities your life has been a disaster. It is not as if you never had the opportunity—your grandson's illness should have melted your iron resolve to have nothing to do with an illegitimate child.

'As the hard person you are we have no alternative but to judge you a failure—a wealthy failure but a failure nevertheless.'

'In the caring world, to which us mere plants belong, your vast wealth means nothing. Sadly it has not even been used to promote well being. When all is said and done what is your money but a number on a piece of paper. Just that.

'Money's true value lies in its use to promote well-being.'

The plants said no more.

He sat there for some time, his mind a blank— They might be right, but he would not accept their condemnation.

'Bloody flowers—I will have the gardeners dig them up tomorrow and dump them on the compost heap. It shouldn't cost much.' Were Harold's last thoughts on this earth.

JML
20/3/2013

THE LUCKIEST MAN ON THE PLANET

*A*s the car sped along the almost empty motorway he turned his mind to his life. He thought that any red-blooded male would envy him. In a word he had it made. He thought that he was the luckiest man on the planet.

Samuel, Sam, Trip was on his way to spend the week-end with one of the sexiest creatures he had ever clapped eyes on. Sharon was absolutely gorgeous, and this was the best bit—she liked him.

They had met at Allan's house. Allan Gibbs was entertaining friends and family to help him celebrate his fiftieth birthday. The atmosphere was lively and the furniture had been removed from one room which was given over to dancing. It was to prove to be a memorable occasion for both Sharon and Sam. The music was modern and the beat persistent. The lighting was low its source hidden from view, and as he made his way amongst the crush of bodies trying to dance he saw her. Their eyes met and her smile almost stopped his heart. He asked her for a dance and she was instantly in his arms. And off they went—spinning round the room locked together and moving as one. Several couples left the floor to simply stand and admire the two figures as they whirled round the now nearly empty dancing area. As they spun he found her body to be lithe and firm and had to resist the urge to fondle her. In the doorway a small crowd had gathered to watch. When there was a pause the music he asked her what she would like to drink. A beer please, she replied as with a wave she acknowledged the mild clapping from the watching group. He soon returned with their drinks and they found a quiet corner in which to get acquainted.

They did not say much—they didn't need to—their display said it all. Later he realised that he was so mesmerised that he could only remember a fraction of what she told him.

It was only several days later, as he was relaxing at home that he realised that he still knew almost nothing about her.

His mind went over the questions—Was she married?
—Divorced?
—A steady boyfriend?
—Did she have a job?
—and if so what was it?
—Did she have a family?
—Why was she at the party on her own?
—Who, if anyone, brought her?
—Was there someone there who had arranged to take her home? If there was, where were they?

These were questions to which he had no answers, and that was then. Now several weeks later he knew little more.

He even went to the extent of phoning Allan and made some enquiries but got nowhere. Allan remembered

interesting step or two. Eventually what happened was inevitable.

He brought the day to mind. It had been hot, very hot, and Angela's folk were on holiday in far away Wales. He had wandered round to the wooden seat on the back awn with a view to giving the Sunday paper a glance. He lt an unexpected thrill as he saw that Angela was in the joining garden. After some time he became aware of a tling coming from over the hedge. Standing up he saw t Angela was struggling to dismantle the collapsible thes carousel and not having much success. In fact she well and truly entangled in the thing together with ral intimate female garments. Only her attractive rear was visible, it was as if the thing was eating her.

Want a lift with that thing?' He shouted over the

es please,' was her muffled reply, 'just go round—the ot locked.'

was easy with two of them, and with the job ne, Angela brought out a couple of dishes of rries and a jar of cream. 'By way of a thank you.' said.

relaxed on a rug strewn with cushions on lawn and chatted about their families. 'I have e photographs of the last holiday we had Angela said 'Would you like to see them?' d yes, and followed her indoors, where it was ly cooler. She led him to a bedroom saying— ry but they are in here, but it is OK please—

turned and gestured for him to follow she ont of the sunlit window, and Sam gasped a

---

the girl but had no idea who had brought her. He had never seem her before—he said. Anyway it was not up to him to tell Sam even if he knew.

A dead end.

Now, here he was—six long weeks later, non the wiser.

Then he had a stroke of luck. Whilst checking pockets of the trousers he was wearing at the party prior to taking them to the cleaners he came upon a scruffy piece of a used table napkin. He was about to discard it when he spotted a number crudely biro's into a corner of it. It looked as if it might be a phone number. On the off chance he tried it—and joy upon joy he recognised the soft female voice answered—

AND MAGICALLY—IT WAS HER.

He suggested dinner at Luigi's and she said that she would like that, and they agreed a time and a date.

He said that he would pick her up at her place, and she gave him an address and directions. It was an occasion that he would never forget. He found that she lived on her own in her well appointed flat. The evening was a great success. They found that she had a wide range of interests many of which they shared. If they had not said much at the party they made up for it then. It was when they returned to her place that to his surprise she dismissed the Taxi and made it abundantly clear that she expected him to stay the night.

There was no doubting that in the absolute physical sense they were totally compatible. They spoke little in the morning. She cooked breakfast and they sat for a long time simply grinning at each other. He formed the impression that she was ready to take him back into the recently vacated bedroom to begin again. But he knew that in spite of a rising desire—it was not in him. They discussed when they might meet again. And eventually he dragged himself away with considerable regret.

It was only several days later, as he was relaxing at home that he realised that he still knew almost nothing about her.

He did however learn that she had a very well paid job in a local government department dealing with the practical side of looking after the annual budget. It was up to her, and her alone, she said to say just how the money was allocated to any given project. Her decisions however had to ratified by the council at the regular budgetary meetings. To-date they had accepted each and everyone of her costed operations.

After this they met several times and in spite of his self doubts the love making simply got better.

It was soon after one such visit to her flat that the subject of vacations dropped naturally into the conversation and Sam chanced his arm.

'Would you consider taking a trip to somewhere warm with me for a week or so?' He asked and held his breath.

Sharon appeared to be considering the prospect.

'Yes,' She said hesitantly, 'but not at sea—I don't like boats.'

'Great, I had somewhere quiet on the Spanish coast in mind.'

And with this memory he reached across the car to the passenger seat to reassure himself of the collection of brochures he had picked up from the agents.

As the miles slid past under his wheels his thoughts were all about Sharon. conversationally she had demonstrated that she possessed a quick mind and had

---

a quirky sense of humour. He chuckled as he rec couple of her rejoinders.

And inevitably he began to dream about her aspects. She was no heavyweight, being fairly sle with a figure that left you in no doubt as to he upper torso was what you would call firm a She had a habit of walking very quickly on th legs which she regarded as an asset and al to show them to their best advantage. By to realise that he was getting physically e considerations, and tried to concentrate which was not at his best.

He couldn't help wishing that he wa but he had a fair way to go yet. Inevit call for fuel at the next service place.

As he arrived there was a small but he was soon clear and his tan parked the car and sought to reliev now, somewhat tired and the self-h In spite of the hurry he was in h doors and got himself a warming

As he plonked himself do noticed a girl who looked rema

The sight of the girl remi one of the luckiest men aliv had wandered into his life.

And what a lovely per her for many years as a fr only recently that they h now adults, and what ha day' kind of thing had g you' kind. In other wor

her glorious figure was suddenly exposed by the strong sun shining through her thin summer garments.

'Are you OK.' Angela asked, 'You have gone a funny colour.' and he got the impression that she was well aware of the situation.

Once in the bedroom she did produce some photographs but it was now far too late, as they sat on the bed he put his arm round her and for the first time he held the lovely weight of her full soft breast and felt the nipple harden under his caress.

He gloried in her wonderful soft roundness, as they explored each other to complete fulfilment.

They were there a long, long time.

And there had been several such occasions since.

As he drove his thoughts were about both girls and he could not help contrasting Angela's soft pneumaticism with Sharon's firm athletic frame.

It was clear that Angela from that moment onwards thought of them as an item, a couple. Whenever they met they made love and it was very satisfying.

So. with not one—but two gorgeous women to make love to he considered that he was a man among men.

Sam was engrossed in these thoughts when it occurred to him that he had better get a move on.

But it was as he was thinking how exciting Angela could be that Sam had a horrible thought. He tried to ignore it—but it would not go away in fact it became more persistent.

He knew that he had arranged separate nights with both women, and had instructed his totally reliable secretary who was sited at firm's head office to make the necessary arrangements whilst he attended the business meeting. It was at a time before mobile phones. She had phoned him back to let him know of the exact times and places. He prided himself on having a good memory, but on this occasion it had let him down. He reflected that he had been distracted whilst she was giving him he information.

His horrified thought was that he had got these arrangements mixed up.

He began to feel sure that he should be heading back the way he had just come, in order to take Angela for an evening meal and an over-night's stay with her.

Damn it he thought. I'm certain that I've got it wrong.

He dare not phone either girl in case he had made a mistake.

He could ring his secretary, but that would take up too much time. No he would just have to turn round and speed back the way he had come.

Back in his car he realised that would have to continue on in the wrong direction until he reached the next turn off which would have a slip road back on to the motorway but now going in the opposite direction. In other words the way he had just come—again.

Risking the police he wound the car up to eighty-five mile per hour, and drove grimly on.

However—

Just then the picture of a naked Sharon popped unasked into his mind, It was now dark—as an early autumn had arrived.

In his overheated imagination she appeared to be dressed in diaphanous flimsy garments and she was reclining invitingly on a bed with black silk sheets.

He screwed up his mind so as to be clear of what he should be doing. If he remembered accurately Angela always did her weekend shopping on this day of the week and thus would be unavailable. So how could he have got it so wrong.

What on earth was he thinking about.

He cursed himself vigorously—but it did no good.

It was a very long way to the next turn off with access back on to the motorway and he knew that he had run out of time.

It was at the same service station that he stopped at last time that he again needed to pay a call. Desperation was setting in and he was still unsure as to the arrangements. He realised that he could loose one or other of the two girls—maybe even both.

Back in the car he held his head in his hands and felt like weeping—he knew that whichever it was he had probably lost the other girl. Both would now wonder what he as playing at.

He decided to simply go home and pretend to be ill.

But too ill to phone?

A decision was required, he would have to bite the bullet and phone one of them, he hoped to find out with which he should be without letting slip that he did not know.

He chose to phone Sharon first.

'Where the hell are you?' Raged a very upset young lady. 'Your secretary said that you were on your way and you know it is my birthday. Don't bother calling

I'll drink the champagne on my own.' And she hung up. Sam's heart sank.

But he rallied and picked up the phone again. This time logic decreed that it must be right.

An equally upset Angela answered on the first ring, she must have been waiting by the phone.

'You have forgotten haven't you?' She said tearfully.

'We were going to tell my parents that we were intending to get engaged. And they have gone to town with the celebrations here. So you can keep the ring.'

And the phone went 'click'.

Sam stood in the cold phone booth for a long, long time. He no longer cared where he was heading—it no longer mattered.

Eventually he simply drove home and went to bed.

He only found out much later that his secretay had been taken ill and had left instructions with the stand-in temp who had got the thing all mixed up and had made both arrangements for the same day.

Sam tried to contact Sharon—he even plucked up the courage and went round to her flat. but it was obvious even from the outside that she no longer lived there.

Her never clapped eyes on her again.

But she is still often in Sam's thoughts when he reflects how it was.

He eventually made it up with Angela, and they now have two children, and he considers himself to be the luckiest man on the planet.

JML
21/3/2013

the girl but had no idea who had brought her. He had never seem her before—he said. Anyway it was not up to him to tell Sam even if he knew.

A dead end.

Now, here he was—six long weeks later, non the wiser.

Then he had a stroke of luck. Whilst checking pockets of the trousers he was wearing at the party prior to taking them to the cleaners he came upon a scruffy piece of a used table napkin. He was about to discard it when he spotted a number crudely biro'd into a corner of it. It looked as if it might be a phone number. On the off chance he tried it—and joy upon joy he recognised the soft female voice answered—

AND MAGICALLY—IT WAS HER.

He suggested dinner at Luigi's and she said that she would like that, and they agreed a time and a date.

He said that he would pick her up at her place, and she gave him an address and directions. It was an occasion that he would never forget. He found that she lived on her own in her well appointed flat. The evening was a great success. They found that she had a wide range of interests many of which they shared. If they had not said much at the party they made up for it then. It was when they returned to her place that to his surprise she dismissed the Taxi and made it abundantly clear that she expected him to stay the night.

There was no doubting that in the absolute physical sense they were totally compatible. They spoke little in the morning. She cooked breakfast and they sat for a long time simply grinning at each other. He formed the impression that she was ready to take him back into the recently vacated bedroom to begin again. But he knew that in spite of a rising desire—it was not in him. They discussed when they might meet again. And eventually he dragged himself away with considerable regret.

It was only several days later, as he was relaxing at home that he realised that he still knew almost nothing about her.

He did however learn that she had a very well paid job in a local government department dealing with the practical side of looking after the annual budget. It was up to her, and her alone, she said to say just how the money was allocated to any given project. Her decisions however had to ratified by the council at the regular budgetary meetings. To-date they had accepted each and everyone of her costed operations.

After this they met several times and in spite of his self doubts the love making simply got better.

It was soon after one such visit to her flat that the subject of vacations dropped naturally into the conversation and Sam chanced his arm.

'Would you consider taking a trip to somewhere warm with me for a week or so?' He asked and held his breath.

Sharon appeared to be considering the prospect.

'Yes,' She said hesitantly, 'but not at sea—I don't like boats.'

'Great, I had somewhere quiet on the Spanish coast in mind.'

And with this memory he reached across the car to the passenger seat to reassure himself of the collection of brochures he had picked up from the agents.

As the miles slid past under his wheels his thoughts were all about Sharon. conversationally she had demonstrated that she possessed a quick mind and had a quirky sense of humour. He chuckled as he recalled a couple of her rejoinders.

And inevitably he began to dream about her physical aspects. She was no heavyweight, being fairly slender, but with a figure that left you in no doubt as to her sex. Her upper torso was what you would call firm and shapely. She had a habit of walking very quickly on those splendid legs which she regarded as an asset and always dressed to show them to their best advantage. By now he began to realise that he was getting physically excited by these considerations, and tried to concentrate on his driving which was not at his best.

He couldn't help wishing that he was already there— but he had a fair way to go yet. Inevitably he needed to call for fuel at the next service place.

As he arrived there was a small queue at the pumps but he was soon clear and his tank was full again. He parked the car and sought to relieve himself. He was, by now, somewhat tired and the self-help cafe attracted him. In spite of the hurry he was in he entered via the swing doors and got himself a warming cup of tea.

As he plonked himself down at a vacant table he noticed a girl who looked remarkably like Angela.

The sight of the girl reminded him as to why he was one of the luckiest men alive. This was because Angela had wandered into his life.

And what a lovely person she was. He had known her for many years as a friend of the family, but it was only recently that they had each noticed that they were now adults, and what had up till then been just a 'Good day' kind of thing had grown with them into a 'how are you' kind. In other words the friendship had taken a more interesting step or two. Eventually what happened was inevitable.

He brought the day to mind. It had been hot, very hot, and Angela's folk were on holiday in far away Wales. He had wandered round to the wooden seat on the back lawn with a view to giving the Sunday paper a glance. He felt an unexpected thrill as he saw that Angela was in the adjoining garden. After some time he became aware of a rattling coming from over the hedge. Standing up he saw that Angela was struggling to dismantle the collapsible clothes carousel and not having much success. In fact she was well and truly entangled in the thing together with several intimate female garments. Only her attractive rear end was visible, it was as if the thing was eating her.

'Want a lift with that thing?' He shouted over the hedge.

'Yes please,' was her muffled reply, 'just go round—the gate's not locked.'

It was easy with two of them, and with the job well done, Angela brought out a couple of dishes of strawberries and a jar of cream. 'By way of a thank you.' She had said.

They relaxed on a rug strewn with cushions on Angela's lawn and chatted about their families. 'I have some nice photographs of the last holiday we had together.' Angela said 'Would you like to see them?'

He said yes, and followed her indoors, where it was considerably cooler. She led him to a bedroom saying—

'I'm sorry but they are in here, but it is OK please—come in.'

As she turned and gestured for him to follow she passed in front of the sunlit window, and Sam gasped as

activities whilst being effectively in disguise. Both sea-goers and townies went at it with a will.

Needless to say these events were not in the original holiday plan.

A group of apes, members of the town band, raided the hotel kitchen and removed a large number of bottles of good wine—these they promptly proceeded to empty by passing the contents down thirsty throats. This lead inevitably to some very high spirited renderings of some well known tunes.

In another quarter of town a small party of large rats broke into the bicycle shop and finding a quantity of trumpets and horns rode through the narrow streets with little care for pedestrians pretending to be the hunt chasing a fox.

The fox however was real, it was the first mate from the ship. He ran as if his life depended on it—which it may well have done.

The local constabulary was overwhelmed by the enormous number of animals. Normally well known characters were now disguised and rubbing shoulders with perfectly innocent party goers.

Then it got ever so slightly more serious—

—Jack Blanche a Woolly Tiger leant backwards over the hotel grill pressed hard in a clinch with a beautifully turned out Badger. Jack's fur caught fire and before he realised it he was well ablaze. The pair of them ran for the pool shouting 'FIRE,' and flung themselves into the water which they entered with a hiss of steam. Unfortunately their dash to safety started several more conflagrations with more party goers joining them in the pool.

All they could do was to watch and to hope that everyone would get to safety.

Just then, our good captain made matters worse by trying to save the ship. He and a stalwart few brave individuals tried to get the ship's fire hoses out, and to start up the pumps to spray the boat and its surroundings with sea water.

The boat was old and its timber dry from days under a hot sun. It burned well.

Everyone did their best but when dawn arrived and they took stock under a terrible black cloud that hung over everything. The sight that met their gaze was ghastly.

The fire spread rapidly to the town which fortunately suffered little serious damage. A coat of paint needed here or there and it would be business as usual.

But of the boat there was absolutely nothing left.

Nothing.

Just a low pile of smoking timbers an a dark smear on the seas sullen surface was all that remained of it.

The locals rallied round. Tables were brought out and food cooked, and coffee or tea made readily available.

But it was some time before it dawned on everyone that the ship's passengers and crew had no clothes. All they had were the ANIMAL COSTUMES, even if some were ever so slightly singed.

So here we have a group of people dressed as snakes, baboons, cats, and you name it, all of no fixed abode wandering vaguely about the town. Fortunately most had some money as they had hidden their credit cards during the conflagration.

The hotels of the town took them in at inflated rates, and very soon the dress and suit shops had nothing to sell except more fancy dress outfits. And pretty soon almost every individual local or visiting was wandering about town in an animal skin.

And it was during the night that the locals seized their opportunity, and a series of robberies and house breakings were investigated by the police who found it impossible to catch and hold anyone when all that was reported was that a baboon grabbed the TV and left in a hurry—

'No I couldn't tell who it was. But he was wearing a baboon skin.'

The police were sad to have to tell the victim that they had twelve baboon cases that morning already. It was a golden opportunity for would be criminals to make themselves rich.

In addition they had cases of people being mugged by tigers.

And break-ins by two polar bears.

And fights by three beavers

Nine giant teddy bears were held, two of which were rapes—alleged.

And a single worm.

Plus a whole herd of drunken donkeys.

In the end they charged no-one, and arrested no-one. After all one gorilla looked much like the any other.

***

Mr Blanch was feeling quite warm in his Gorilla skin, as he wandered along almost deserted streets in town looking for that slick tuna fish he had caught a glimpse of as she struggled to adopt the suit, she was completely naked underneath that silvery shell.

Unfortunately she was being chased by our captain who had assumed that he outranked all other males and as the girl was trying to don the skin he was endeavouring to remove it.

It started fight which very soon had two tigers, five bulldogs, and a giraffe all joined in.

A police car soon arrived just as the party broke up and those involved melted into the gathering throng.

Another defeat for law and order.

Miss Alice Tugworthy, a stern and forbidding librarian back home, decided not to miss this opportunity of a lifetime to catch up with everyone else. And now there she was in a semi transparent worm costume gyrating in a dance of erotic proportions.

As she did she made it plain that she would sacrifice herself to the young and very handsome lad gazing at her with open mouth.

A pair of pigs all pink with jolly grinning faces were trying to negotiate a bed for the night for themselves at a small hotel near the square.

As you can see there were many persons—some intent on crime others keen to take full advantage of the situation and slake their base desires.

It was a time to remember with everyone taking full advantage of the imposed situation.

It went on ALL NIGHT

Two days later the Town Mayor called a council meeting and tried to ignore the fact that half the council were still dressed as animals. Several were also nursing very bad booze induced headaches.

To say that the Mayors good wife was not very good looking would be to understate the fact by a large margin. Her looks had in fact been known to frighten small children and subdue grown men. She had not joined in but had observed the goings on with increasing disapproval from their bedroom window.

So over their breakfast she ranted and raved at the Mayor for allowing such freedom. The poor chap had no chance to retaliate as she left no gaps in her condemnation. She had clearly decided that the whole thing was his fault. And so she charged him with urgently calling a council meeting with the clear object of stopping such a thing happening again.

The Mayor felt that he had little choice—he therefore called an urgent council meeting, this behaviour must prevented if he were to get any peace at all at home.

They met with some reluctance on the councillor's part, and they faced the Mayor with truculent faces.

The Mayor assumed all the dignity he could muster, and in his sternest voice he said—

'What happened last night was dreadful.' He emphasised his words by thumping the table.

'It is a stain on the town's reputation, and we must ensure that such a thing never, ever happens again. Therefore I propose that the Council establish a ban on all fancy dress costumes being worn in the streets at any time—night or day, with stiff penalties for all offenders.

He gazed round the gathering with a look of considerable triumph. And with tremendous confidence said—

—'So all in favour raise your hands.'-

BUT TO HIS ASTONISHMENT—NO-ONE MOVED,

After an expectant and lengthy pause a Goat stood up, coughed nervously, and replied—'On the contrary, we should hold an annual Grand Town Party. Fancy dress only to be worn, penalties to be applied to any-one not wearing a costume.'

His audience, apart from the Mayor, exhibited grins.

'Further, it should be held in mid-summer, and last for two whole consecutive days and nights. Food and drink to be free—paid for out of the town funds—.'

Cheers greeted this, as all those present, except the Mayor, acknowledged their fervent support for this new proposal.

In spite of the Mayors futile attempt to prevent it, it was duly written into the meeting minutes and it has since become a very famous world-wide attraction.

The Mayor's wife insisted that he resigned.

Our tourists were eventually repatriated and most of them applied to go again the very next year.

JML
8/4/2013

?**?**??

THE GIRL IN QUESTION

*I*t was only the slightest of fleeting glimpses, but it stayed with him for the whole of the rest of his long life.

His train was early arriving at York where it halted to exchange passengers. He looked up from the book he was reading and glanced out of the window. His view of a busy railway station was suddenly interrupted as the gap between him and the platform was filled by another train slowly coming to a stop.

It came to rest with a high pitched squeal of brakes. And in that instant he knew that his life would never be the same. Her eyes met his and his heart turned a summersault. She was sat in the window seat which came to rest exactly opposite his own. They were in sight of each other for just about two very short minutes before his train slowly moved off gathering speed as it went. The shock left him numb and for some time he was unable to think coherently. As his train accelerated round the tight bend that would take her away for ever the carriage's flanged wheels screeched their protest and it was only then as the train left the station that normal thought processes returned to him.

And these thoughts were about, what else?—But The Girl.

It was not that she was especially good looking in the conventional sense. Taken individually each item—eyes, nose, mouth etcetera seemed to be unexceptional. It was that the total effect of all the parts taken together which amounted to what he considered to be the most attractive thing he had seen in his whole short life.

Strangely her expression was of recognition which somehow led him to believe that she instantly returned his feelings, there was a promise, however ridiculous, in her eyes that said that she understood and felt exactly the same.

As he realised this and considered that which he had just found and within the space of two very short minutes lost again for ever. He now knew deep within his inner self that this binding force of passion, of a true and all embracing love might never now be his—in that intense moment she had stolen it.

He was immediately consumed by two powerful and opposite sensations. One was that he had seen what deep love might really be like, and the other—that it may never now be his. He had lost it, he might one day have owned it, but now it might never be. It felt to him that it really had gone.

Gone. The word echoed round his brain.

However—his journey still had a couple of hours to run and the intense emotion of the past few minutes had left him tired and depressed, and he drifted into a deep and dreamless sleep.

As he slept the image of The Girl burned itself into the cells of his brain. It was so powerful an image that it actually modified some of the more important strands of his DNA. In other words he was no longer the person who boarded the five-fifteen to Newcastle Upon Tyne. There were subtle changes to the person he had been. He was of coarse unaware of this modification but from now on The Girl's (or the image of her) had an influence on his thinking and thus in certain cases his actions without his realising it.

How this worked out we shall see.

***

He was awakened by a friendly shake of his arm.

'We are at the terminus, Sir, we don't go any farther—would you like some help with your luggage?'

'Is this Newcastle then?'

'It is sir. We have just arrived, Seven minutes early.' He announced. A measure of pride in his voice.

John Wendover thanked the guard, gathered his luggage off the rack and made his way to the door and out onto the crowded, busy and noisy platform to join the rest of the people also making their way towards the exit. At the barrier their tickets were not requested, and quite suddenly he found himself outside on a very busy street with a long queue for taxis.

He was somewhat surprised that it was still broad daylight. At home, London would be quite dark by now.

The Company had arranged his accommodation and he spelled out the address to the driver who helped him load the luggage, saw him comfortably seated, and slowly drove out into the evening traffic.

***

John had never been to this part of Britain before and whilst being apprehensive at the newness of it all, he was looking forward to the change of environment.

Newcastle-upon-Tyne was, by all accounts, a very different place, to his home environment. And here he now was, at last.

As the cab took him through the town he was intrigued to see that the streets were crowded with people—many of whom were dressed as if for a fancy dress party.

There was a group of nuns whose demeanour was far from nun-like.

A pair of bears appeared strolling along arm in arm.

Saturday night was obviously party night in Newcastle. He made his mind up to sample some of it. It was as if the place was welcoming him.

The memory of the incident with The Girl was temporarily forced to the back of his mind as he absorbed all that was happening around him. The place that was to become his home city for a considerable time.

Flat number 33 was just one of many in a fairly large red brick block, but he found it very much to his taste, sort of mid nineteen-fifties. The taxi man dumped his gear just inside the door, and stood clearly awaiting a good tip. Once alone John began to explore his temporary home.

The company he was now employed by as a sales representative had moved his territory from his home patch of Manchester to Newcastle. He was charged with creating a strong sales force to replace the existing one which appeared to be failing. It was a continuing surprise to him that so much business could result from selling buttons. Granted the company currently marketed the widest range of buttons sold anywhere in the UK. They ranged from the standard white pearl shirt fasteners to enormous fancy ones made out of translucent plastic—a statement on a woman's fancy top. They even had ones which could be lit by means of a tiny flashing light.

John knew that the job would be uphill to start with, and was prepared to succeed, his aim being to make his mark on the team and to help them become the companies number one sales force.

He had to prove it to the company and especially to himself.

Satisfied by his brief check round that everything seemed to be working OK, he dug a bottle of Red Grouse out of his luggage, switched on the box and nestled into one of the easy chairs opposite, and for the first time relaxed.

The Girl was forgotten as the whiskey took its effect and he dozed as the news burbled inconsequentially out from the now totally ignored TV.

It was much later when he eventually nestled down in the soft bed warmed by its electric blanket that she appeared.

Suddenly—Unsolicited, a clear image of The Girl took over his mind. So realistic was this that he tried, in his sleep, to reach out across the gap between their trains to touch her. He very nearly succeeded when with an awakening bang he landed on the floor beside the bed.

Disoriented at first he wondered where the other train was. Fortunately he suffered only mild bruises.

But the incident deprived him of sleep for the rest of the night.

John was thankful that next day was Sunday, and with any luck he should have recovered something of his usual equanimity in good time to face the sales team on the forthcoming Monday. However not wanting to start by getting involved in the business of preparing a midday meal for himself he followed his natural instinct and walked the short distance to the pub he had spotted from the taxi.

There were few people about and an almost complete absence of traffic.

The Blaydon Castle was one of those timeless hostelries favoured only by locals and stacked with a host of its own unwritten rules. It was early hours when he pushed open the doors and found himself in another world.

The bar room was packed, almost every seat at every table taken, the atmosphere thick with smoke.

There was a sort of hush as he made his way to the bar, but the prevailing sense was that the crowd were friendly rather than hostile. He ordered a Newcastle Brown. The first he had ever tried, and was surprised that it was delivered as a bottle and an empty half pint glass.

He was even more surprised when a comely lass got his attention.

'There's not much room, but y'can an sit with us if ye like.' She said waving to one of the empty seats.

'Thank you.' He replied, 'I never though it would be so busy,'

'Eye man, it always is on a Sunda.' She returned.

They did their best to involve him but the accent and the language defeated him.

When the food man came round they placed an order for food for him—A ham stottie, which was good boiled ham in a sandwich made with a rather large triangular bun, served with a pile of spicy pickle

In spite of the language problem he managed to enjoy himself, and several 'Newkies' later he thanked his new friends and made his way back to the flat.

It was a promising start.

He decided on a shower to remove the smell of the pub, and it was as he was combing his hair the face that smiled back at him from the mirror was that of The Girl. But before he could say or do anything she faded as the mirror steamed up.

Suddenly feeling very tired he put his stuff for tomorrow together and retired to bed where he slept dreamlessly. It had been a long day, in which he began to recognise that this place was very different from what he had been used to.

***

Monday—the day he would meet the team.

He took a Taxi across town to the meeting venue, after solving the problem of getting the taxi driver to understand where he wanted to go.

The Hotel was large and modern and the desk clerk was ready for him and the lift took him to the room. The group were already seated in easy chairs and drifted into an expectant silence.

'Good morning,' he began, conventionally enough. His greeting was returned

And they were silent—waiting. Just what would this new guy bring. Clearly he was here to make a difference, after all the sales figures had recently been quite dreadful—hence this new boss. Anyone could see that there would be changes.

'Now, I hope to get to know you but in the meantime could you take it in turn to state your name and how long you have been with the company? Starting with you—' He said nodding to the you lad nearest to him.

It broke the ice and he was able to make them laugh with one or two rather obvious jokes.

Then—

'Now for the bad news—this week's targets. As you will see they have been increased over last years for the same period. And this is in spite of your own expectation of less.' This produced the expected groan. John at that point stuck a sheet on the wall which gave the new targets for each of them. They groaned again although most of them had 'saved' a few sales from the previous week by simply not declaring them and would meet the new targets with a bit of luck and a following wind. But what about the month after?

It all went very well, and the formal meeting ended at lunch time when the whole team retired to the Blaydon Castle for a bite and a pint, and to discus rumours and moans.

They had been so busy that The Girl had not once entered his mind.

He learned that their previous boss was well thought of by the team. They had thought that he was going places and was in line for promotion when he would be re-allocated to London.

Quite early in the evening by Newcastle standards John excused himself pleading journey tiredness and left them to it.

Back in the peace of his hotel room he looked at his short list of prospective clients who fell into his nominated territory, and was satisfied that he was as well organised as it was possible to be.

It was as he was drifting into sleep that her face appeared, and once again her sheer beauty as she smiled at him overwhelmed every other thought.

***

It was the first thing he was aware of as he awoke in unfamiliar surroundings and sounds—the smell of cooked bacon. He spent a few minutes re-orienting himself before launching himself out of bed and into the day.

The first job was to pick up the company car from the nearby garage—He liked it immediately—especially as it had an automatic gearbox.

His first client had a small chain of DIY dress shops and the nice mature proprieties gave him a substantial order—it was a good start.

The hotel had provided him with sandwiches which he ate sitting in the car overlooking the Tyne as it flowed black and sluggishly past.

It would become a critical item, a symbol, in his life.

The Tyne. The result of the joining together of the river North Tyne and The River South Tyne. His territory spanned parts of both North and South Shields in the arms of which the Tyne gathered in the sea.

That evening would be taken up with a follow-up team meeting at his hotel and at which they would discuss ways and means of increasing sales. His team was currently running eighth in the company's achievement list, which was considered to be a very poor performance.

The area, the company reckoned, was capable of a much better result.

This had led to their manager being given one more chance to do better—He had failed, a new manager—John—had been taken on. So for him and them it was all new.

The team arrived one by one and made their way through the swing doors. At the reception desk they was given the room number and were directed to the lift.

The chosen room was light and airy and the ten who made up the team group settled themselves round the central table and producing their paperwork.

The last of them in place, John called the meeting together and asked them why the team's results were so poor when the potential of the area was so much greater.

This was greeted by a stony silence. They had not expected such a direct approach.

Fortunately tea arrived and general chit-chat took over. John felt that he had to find the weaknesses and put a recovery plan into force, and speedily. John startled them all by announcing his own target which was short and to the point. It was simply to make the team THE COMPANY'S MOST SUCCESSFUL TEAM And he shook them by stating that anyone who failed in this task would be asked to leave the company. There was no compromise or comfort in the message. They were being told to succeed or go.

A very sober group of individuals left the hotel now considerably nervous about their prospects.

***

Later in his hotel room with a welcome cup of warming tea John tried to feel good about the future, but was far from confident—the rest of them already knew their territory whereas he had to start to build his market from scratch. He felt that he would be given no special consideration for this. It was starting to look as if he might do his best and still fail.

All he had was a list of potential customers left by the previous owner of the job.—It was not long and should have been longer, he would have to re-assess the area and scout hard for new buyers. It was his prevailing thought as he drifted into sleep.

***

The rest of that first week drifted by with enormous speed. At the end of it he had added two more clients to the list and had obtained three or four good orders.

He was so intensely occupied that the girl's image never once made an appearance. It was time to meet and put a team plan together.

This time it was more business-like and they were able to target fresh customers and develop new ways of attracting more business from their existing clients.

It was a time of great progress the company were introducing a brand new portfolio of exciting buttons— it was recognised that this was the best in the industry and the team were keen to get hold of samples. John gave himself this task as a priority.

But there was a flaw in their plans in the shape of a rival company making a bid for the self same market.

At the end of the first month their results were well below the target. London were not pleased.

A new-comer was sent to put things right.

The meeting sat waiting for this high level company trouble shooter.

They were quiet—subdued.

A knock on the door and in a walked greatest shock of John's whole life.

So what was it?

Well even now it is difficult to put it into words, but the effect on John was devastating.

This individual was tall with a woman's figure. Dressed as a man in a suit and tie he strode into the room and flung his brief case onto the table and glared around—he was not there to be nice.

And shockingly for John—*IT WAS THE GIRL*.

He had no doubts—the image was burnt into his brain and there it was the real thing just as it had been on the train.

Eyes, nose, lips, chin, ears and hair—Jackie was she. There was no room for doubt.

Jackie Lee addressed John with a detached look and made it clear that ultimately he, John was responsible for the team's overall performance.

The emotions surging round in John nearly overwhelmed him, and it was only with a tremendous effort he managed to avoid passing out.

Jackie Lee noticed the effect that his words had on John, indeed they were soon to discover that in the case of Jackie almost nothing was not seen, noted, and stored for future use.

John apologised, and this was accepted with a nod.

'Now to business,' said Jackie, 'I assume that you have with your staff here ironed out a business plan?' It was a statement not a question.

'Er no.' John said sheepishly, 'there hasn't really been time.'

Jackie looked horrified.

'So just when did you propose to do this work then.?' It was a question but it sounded more like a criticism.

'Well,—er now.' responded John.

'So go ahead then, ignore me Jackie said. And he/she waved a hand at John.

John turned to the member of his group whom he had already earmarked to be his second in command. 'Lets begin with a list of all likely purchasers in your area. I assume you do have such a list.'

'I was about to place such a document before you.' He produced a largish sheet covered in small figures each of which carried a number.

That number is an assessment of order we would hope to obtain.'

'STOP' shouted Jackie.

'This is all very nice and cosy—but what I want to see is our customers listed in team order, and columns headed "last order/ date / size" then "next order forecast date/ size." That way we can monitor everyone's performance. And by the way you can forget bonuses until this begins to produce results.'

He gazed round at glum faces, stood up, and made his way to the door, remarking as he went.

'We will meet again here in one week's time, and remember John that it is your neck that is on the block.'

And the door swung shut, leaving behind a room full of stunned and very unhappy individuals.

John spent the rest of the meeting trying to draught the document as described by Jackie.

It took a long time and they were busy well into the night.

They were so busy in fact that John had no time to consider his reaction to the 'Girl/Man'.

Later in the local over a couple of Newky-browns with several team members John considered the problem. He found that about one third of the team thought that Jackie was essentially a man wanting to be a woman, one third thought that she was a woman playing the part of a man. The rest were unsure and chose to await events.

Back in his room John was horrified by the events of the day. The effect on him whenever their eyes met was to turn his heart to jelly. He was not so much in love, he was totally smitten.

As for the job—he recognised the ruthless core of Jackie who would blame him for any failure, and ensure his removal from his position without any consideration, should he fail in Jackie's eyes.

Strangely—in spite of his stomach churning feelings for Jackie with the breathtaking beauty—he found that he detested intensely that cruel personality he/she had shown him/herself to be.

It was with this dilemma churning round inside his head that he eventually drifted in and out of a disturbed sleep.

***

And it got worse—much worse.

The target chart was produced and judged by Jackie to be nowhere good enough. Target levels were ridiculously low he/she said.

'If we go with this the company will be bankrupt before the end of the month. Just what the hell were you thinking of John—the targets should be doubled AT LEAST.' He/she shouted this.

'But what if the business just isn't there,' John attempted to defended himself.

'Don't you dare say that in front of the team you idiot—they need a challenge.'

'This is not a challenge it's an impossibility.' said John.

'By god—if you say that again I will have you out.'

John was an very unhappy individual.

He was desperately in love with the way that the female Jackie looked, he could not see enough of him/her. But he detested that individual at the same time for his/her attitude to himself and the team—which he thought was counter productive.

John's second Newcastle month was coming to an end and it was clear that the new targets would again not be met by a significant margin.

Jackie again arrived on the scene for a one on one meeting with John.

It was a disaster.

'So what the hell do I tell our masters back in London? They will want a sacrifice and I will make sure that it is you.' Jackie raged at John.

John was plagued by the love-hate feelings he had for Jackie but he had been pushed too far.

With a desperate struggle he had until now managed to keep himself under some sort of control

'We cannot achieve that which is just not possible and with your attitude towards me—you are in danger of forcing me to do something drastic.'

John raged at Jackie.

'You seem to have forgotten where you are—you are very far from London and the people here are tough and very rough.

Many a corpse has drifted out to sea carried on the waters of the Tyne never to be seen again—it can easily be arranged. It happens all the time. And who in London would give a damn?'

It was showdown time.

Jackie was red with unsuppressed rage.

'How dare you threaten me. I have the support of the management and I'll have you torn to pieces and chucked out of the company.'

They sat and glared at each other, neither of them daring to pull that final trigger.

Suddenly and unexpectedly Jackie shoved his papers back into his brief case, and he/she smiled and a beautiful smile it was. It set John's heart into spasms.

And then in a quiet new voice he/she said—

'Perhaps we should go out and have dinner somewhere expensive, on the firm.'

This was nearly too much for John. What was going on. What game was Jackie playing.

It took him some time to realise that he had nothing to loose as Jackie would see to it that he was kicked out of the firm. So full of suspicion he agreed.

As they were leaving the hotel Jackie asked the manager which was the very best eating place in town. He sent them to a very expensive restaurant specialising in fish dishes, somewhere north of Newcastle.

Once seated and having placed their order as advised by the head waiter and the chef, by mutual agreement they did not discuss business matters for fear of ruining the taste of an excellent repast.

It was a struggle for John at first as strong emotions were still raging in his breast. But they found a common interest in European holidays—mostly Italy of which they had both explored and enjoyed.

John found that Jackie had an almost infinite list of amusing tales of holiday incidents, which despite his suspicions had him roaring with genuine laughter. The meal came to an end and Jackie signed the bill for an amount that astonished John.

In the taxi which Jackie ordered to take them back to John's hotel, John found that on balance he had enjoyed himself—and that meal really was something else.

Back in John's rooms Jackie revealed more of a tender, fun loving side to is nature, which deepened John's suspicion.

But then quite suddenly and unexpectedly Jackie burst into tears.

And a couple of stiff whiskies later he showed John that he was not happy with the company, and that he was certain that they were trying find a reason to sack him, hence the impossible targets.

After further revelations, it seemed to be natural to both of them that Jackie should stay the night.

At sometime later that night John found Jackie full of surprises.

The following morning they were both shy of each other. However in the tentative discussion over coffee the atmosphere warmed and soon became animated as they gained confidence. When the team plan was brought up it was clear that neither of them believed in it.

They never remembered afterwards who mentioned it first but the fact of resigning came up. Giving each other the necessary courage they both set about writing their resignations with immediate effect.

With that decision taken and effectively put into action they relaxed and began the long pleasurable process of getting to know each other. Monday they would set out to try and obtain re-employment, but it was Sunday and a day on the coast was just what they needed to seal their relationship. They had just one more meeting with the team.

They were somewhat relieved that the targets would be eased, and promised to give the pair help in finding suitable employment.

It took a while but with the team's contacts the pair were soon fixed—They started a business selling, of all things—buttons.

Was Jackie a he or a she? They found that it really did not matter—but in point of fact he/she was just exactly that.

JML
27/6/2013

OF GOLDEN HAIR

*E*ven though it was the thousandth time,
  It was just the same as the first.
  His mind's image was as clear as if she were still there—
  In his inner eyes—
  Straw coloured hair swept up high and held,
  Was how it usually was;
  Occasionally she would tease it loose and free,
  And then she was Boticcelli's Venus rising from the
blue ocean sea.
  Then this enchanting face,
  Was surrounded by a glorious shimmering cascade
of gold.
  Her hair a treasure to behold.
  And who could ignore those brilliant green eyes,
  Of unfathomable depths.
  Eyes which hinted of a life—beyond life.
  Of sights better remain unspoken.
  Those eyes which told—
  "I can see into your very soul, and I will judge you."
  And I wondered again for the thousandth time, just
what secrets they had seen.

———————

Her nose matched well defined soft lips.

Which if not displaying an inviting smile—

Appeared to be about to part offering the softest of kisses.

For him her slightly wanton gaze could not be matched—

Here was lust only just held under control, or so he imagined.

His heart raced in his breast—

As it had when first he saw her,

And always since in his dreams and waking moments.

***

There was no pattern to her appearances nor any hints. Suddenly she was there.

As he sat gazing at the screen, hands on the keyboard, she might appear un-announced, breaking his train of thought, interrupting the work in progress, and demanding his whole attention.

Then came that fateful day, without warning, when he could do nothing until he had spoken to her and he realised that he had no idea as to how this might be achieved.

In all this time he and she had never had a proper conversation—it was always she who spoke, and when she did it would be about something of little consequence.

She would appear—smiling, and as lovely as ever.

'Good morning Alfred—you look well today. I hope you slept well.'

Or—'It looks as if the weather forecasts might be correct—we might just have some more snow.'

He knew that she could see him via the web-cam—

'You look a little pale this morning. I hope that you are not coming down with something.'

Or again—'I am sorry but I don't like the tie you've chosen for today—It really doesn't go with that shirt.'

This last remark caused him to check how he looked every day just in case it was one of her appearances.

It did not seem to him as strange that he should be acting this way to what was only a computer image.

However he tried always to look his best when on the machine. And it paid off. Her criticisms gradually changed to compliments.

'You look nice today, I always liked that shirt.'

So far he had only listened to her—too fascinated to speak, but the questions were piling up as well they might.

Who was she?

How did she get into his machine?

Could she hear him?

He had only seen her head and face—what was the rest of her like?—

***

Eventually, after some months he admitted to himself that this computer driven image of an attractive girl had become important to him, much as a real person might.

Somehow he felt that if she were to allow him increased contact it would lead to a situation over which he had no control, but at the same time that she would involve him deeply in her world eventually allowing him no means of escape.

He felt that she was very subtly gaining control over him.

He tried to ignore her interruptions.

There was a deadline to meet if he were to get paid for the work he was struggling to complete.

It was not always the same, but typically he would be composing a business letter perhaps re-arranging one of his many investments, fingers hammering on the letters on the key board. He was neither a fast nor particularly accurate typist and had to concentrate hard to get it right without having to stay up all night to get it finished.

Then, without warning, the sentence he was in the middle of typing would begin to waver and to fade. The screen would gradually become simply plain and single coloured, and no matter how many keys he pressed it would not go away. Then a cloud would form which finally resolved itself into her.

And as she smile a welcome his heart would race and his mind would empty of all else.

His fingers would automatically press the keys which allowed her image to completely fill the screen. He could see that she was in a garden. Flowers in the background, on a window ledge behind her, wavered—gently moved by a light breeze.

He waited.

On this occasion like many others she did not speak.

After a while the image faded, to leave his mind puzzling hard and all his emotions in turmoil.

Had his computer been invaded?

Was she real or was the image merely the result of some clever software which had taken over his system?

Or was she simply the product of a lonely mind. HIS mind.

His questions were many.

But of answers there were none.

**

For some unfathomable reason he did not want to share her with anyone else, so for the time being at least he kept her existence to himself. It was not that he feared that they might think he was just making it up, or that he was simply day dreaming, or worse—going crackers. It was more of a question of someone pinching her from him.

Then it became serious—It began to have a detrimental affect on his work, and this began to worry him which in turn began affect his health.

He decided to break the routine—He planned a holiday.

Some time away from his blasted computer.

He hoped that this would break the spell. It had to be a break that would keep him busy and his mind one hundred percent occupied.

He chose a skiing holiday—he would learn to ski.

Before he could change his mind he had booked a holiday in Scotland travelling by coach and residing for seven days at a well known hotel somewhere in the Glen Coe district where they specialised in training beginners to ski. Although on his own the rest of the hotel guests, also learning to ski, were very friendly and he was not bothered by images on a computer screen of dazzling young females. He felt free and hoped that it would remain so when he was back home.

He thoroughly enjoyed his skiing experience and the company of the other guests. Every day was full from waking to sleeping. And to his surprise he became quite a reasonably skier. At the end of his stay they had an

Awards Day at which he was presented with a prize for the most improved student.

There was however, a strange ephemeral feeling that he was not quite in control. It was as if he were acting to someone else's script. Even his attempts to talk to the other guests were as if he was not responsible for the words.

This external agency seemed to be with him all the time, but vanished if he tried to get to it.

He returned back home where he lived on his own in a small two story detached house which had been presented to him by a wealthy aunt who said the it was surplus to her requirements.

Strangely he remembered nothing of the return journey—just plain nothing—zero, zilch. One minute he was returning his skis to the hotel store, the next he was strolling in through his familiar front door.

However, he now felt that he had to meet The Girl, as he had come to know her, face to face.

On arrival at the house he was invaded by a strange and unsettling sensation that it was as if he had not been anywhere. But that the whole episode was simply put together in his computer. Or even worse—had only existed in his mind. The other disturbing feeling was the return of an incredible desire to see 'The Girl' again.

He dumped his luggage in the hall and dashed into the computer room where he flung himself at the machine and pressed the buttons to bring the thing to life. He scorned himself even as he did this.

The machine gradually displayed its start-up images and he went through the routine of connecting it to the network.

He sat there and waited but of the girl there was no sign—just the usual list of his files.

Perhaps if he began to work?

He slammed the keys.

Nothing.

He thrashed the keyboard for over an hour.

Nothing.

He switched off—waited for the software to settle—Switched on, and pressed the keys again.

Nothing.

Perhaps the machine was not working.

He called up some much used files, and found that he could amend these.

OK—

So the thing was working. He pressed keys that previously had resulted in The Girl's appearance.

Nothing.

He tried all the keys and combinations, but to all intents and purposes she had gone.

He decided to try again the next day and switched off and watched the machine close down in its usual methodical manner.

Time to think?

He had a restless night.

He dreamed of her—what else?

He awoke and hoped to come to the problem refreshed.

***

However in the cold light of dawn he began to get the feeling that he was missing some vital clue. Something obvious—

But what?

He tried to analyse what he knew about The Girl. Just how was it that she came to his screen un-called for.

Who was she? Where did she live? And critically—how on earth did she know so much about him? How did she access his machine. Above all—WAS SHE REAL or just a half remembered remembered image? From some dream.

He decided to write down all the facts as he saw them.

It took a while but eventually he finished up with twenty A4 sheets of closely typed text.

He read this through several times and very gradually began to recognise that he was missing that one valuable clue, something so simple and basic as to be easily overlooked.

Interestingly he felt that what was missing was to do with himself and not The Girl.

Because it made no sense as it was, he resolved to go over the whole thing again.

Then, out of the blue she was suddenly there on his screen.

And she spoke.

'Where have you been for the last fortnight,' she asked. 'I looked everywhere but couldn't find you.'

'I was on holiday,' he replied.

But as he said this he felt that there was more to the fact than he was able to say or even to understand.

Over all this to-ing and fro—ing there was some fundamental issue that governed all that had happened that he was still missing.

'It is late,' she said 'get some sleep—understanding may come with the morning. You are shutting out the answer to it all.'

'I will see you tomorrow—Good Night.'

The image died before he could press the keys to shut down and the screen went blank.

***

The following day—

On awaking he felt that after today things would never be the same again.

To is surprise the machine was on when he entered the computer room.

He was pretty certain that he had switched it off the previous night.

He sat in front of the screen fingers on the key board.

Then whilst he was again pondering how to raise The Girl—There she was.

Her hair was loose and she had little make up on.

He thought that he had never seen her look so attractive. So sure, So relaxed—and wearing that captivating smile.

'Good morning,' she said—'I hope that you will still be my friend after this.'

'Of course I will.' He replied with more conviction than he felt.

What was this revelation that she thought would be so horrifying as to end their relationship?

'Right,' she said,

'So you feel in control?'

'Yes,' he said.

'OK, then change just one small thing like the background colour to the picture on the screen. From green to red say.'

HE FOUND THAT HE COULD NOT. No matter what he tried.

'But I can,' she said—watch.'

The screen became bathed in a red glow.

His mind would not accept the reality of it.

'Yes,' she said, 'it is you who are a computer image, and it is me who is pressing the keys.'

For some time nothing happened.

'I am sorry if this is a shock but rest assured you and I will continue to work together.'

He had no words to describe his feelings.

Where there was once life—now there was just a dead picture on a computer screen.

Then as he struggled to come to terms with this terrible fact—his total existence depended on The Girl.

It would clearly take some getting used to.

Life as he once knew it was no longer available to him,

But then it suddenly dawned on him—it should not be possible—BUT HE WAS STILL CAPABLE OF INDEPEND THOUGHT

—and there was still The Girl.

It might not be quite so bad. After all.

JML
15/5/2013

STICK

$\mathcal{I}$t is now lost to human memory and will remain thus for ever just how Stick acquired the name. You see, although it was just a stick, an every day object, it had a name just like you and I. And its name was Stick.

Thus it would be quite incorrect to say 'Did you come with a stick.' In this case one should say 'Is Stick with you?'

You see the difference?

It was Wondred Tyler who became Stick's closest friend sharing with him, as he, did, a large detached house in the suburbs of one of our larger cities. Opposite their house grew a deep and seriously dense wood. Wondred and Stick would take full advantage of any fine weather to take an early morning stroll along the path that meandered along the edge of the wood.

Stick loved these walks, especially in the seasons of the trees—spring, summer and autumn, and if the weather was settled and fine would convey his need to be out there strolling through the woods. This desire to be out and about was shared between them, and Wondred would feel that same thrill coursing through his limbs, and grabbing Stick he would be off to return after a good hour or so stride.

So how did Wondred know what Stick wanted?

This is not known, although studies have shown that some form understanding did exist between them.

***

It was November the fifth, Bonfire Night, and Stick had not yet been claimed. For the previous several days the local lads had been out and about grabbing any unwanted timber for the bonfire. They built this wood into a single large heap which now stood about as high as a tall man. On his own Wondred was taking an early evening stroll through the wood when he came across one of these stacks of loose branches waiting for the torch to turn it into a bonfire. Near the top of the stack was a good looking stave, unusually straight and sound. As Wondred was striding past some secret thing, an animal or a sharp breeze moved touched the branch altering the delicate balance that had hitherto remained unchanged and our stave became dislodged from its position near the top of the stack and slid down in such a manner as to come to rest standing upright supported in that position by the other lengths of branch.

A startled Wondred stopped to look at this unusual thing.

He studied the branch and concluded that when its unwanted side shoots had been removed it would make a very fine stick.

It would be a stick that Wondred thought that he could walk with and not feel like an old man.

It was then just a matter of moments for him to wrest the branch from the stack. When he got it clear it was even better—being dead straight, about the right length, and very strong.

Back at the house Wondred removed the unwanted side branches, and cleaned the one which was left.

Wondred had his stick.

It was with the natural passage of time and some very unusual happenings that Wondred's stick began to appear to take on some of the attributes of a human personality.

Memory of the first of such occasions is now lost to the insistence of time's progress. But at some point the stick appeard to exhibit human-like actions of its own.

**

The earliest recollection of something odd was noticed not by Wondred but by an acquaintance who was on this walking holiday in the Lake District with him.

They had opted to climb that grand old mountain Helvellyn via Striding edge.

It was as they were negotiating that final almost vertical thrust of rock that led to relatively level ground of the top that it happened. Wondred was on this final scramble, when the ground underneath him gave way and he began a deadly slide off the mountain.

Fortunately he had his stick with him and he had thrust it into the ground ahead of himself to leave his hands free but the stick was now well out of his reach. To the observer's amazement the stick spun in the air and came down not just within reach but also jammed between a pair of large boulders. It then only took a moment for Wondred to reach out, grab this life saver, and haul himself to safety.

Our observer feeling that he would be laughed at, never mentioned the strange fact of the stick's strange action to anyone except Wondred, who simply said that he had also witnessed it, and looked puzzled. He held the stick out to his companion who took it somewhat nervously and examined it thoroughly.

'Its just a stick,' he said handing it back.

**

Later that same year Wondred and a couple of mates, namely Frank and Robin found themselves on a walking holiday in Snowdonia in N. Wales. Deep in those grand mountains a thick mist descended and they found themselves lost. They had a map but no compass and Satnav had not yet been invented, they had no idea which route would take them safely down to the pub.

Wondred suddenly felt a strong tug on the stick. He was taken unawares and almost let go of the stick. But as the tug got stronger he had no choice but to follow the way the thing was pulling him. This was observed by his companions who decided that they had little choice but to trust Wondred and his cane.

Several miles later they dropped out of the mist to find themselves on one side of a stone wall on the other side of which was the main road.

And the pub and safety.

Saved by a piece of wood—it did not seem likely. But again the stick's action had witnesses.

However there was as yet insufficient such actions to recognise that there was something very special with Wondred's chunk of wood.

But those who had seen it in action developed a natural respect for its possible powers.

***

But then there was the case of Sandy. Sandy had broken some bones in her foot whilst ice skating. She had crashed into a tree whose branches protruded up through the ice and were now well and truly frozen in. To the astonishment of the many gathered onlookers. This stick, which had been laid on the ground whilst Wondred fastened his shoe laces, slid itself across the gap between the girl and the bank where Wondred picked up the free end and hauled the girl to safety.

Wondred, hero of the moment, answered the many question thrown at him with the simple statement that it was just luck that his stick rolled down the bank when it did. But now more people had witnessed something very strange.

***

Then near disaster—the press found out that there was in their midst a piece of a tree that did extraordinary things. So to escape awkward questions to which he had no answer For a time Wondred took a holiday.

He went to Australia, and he took his stick.

It was when they visited a remote settlement of original Australians that things got really interesting.

You see the cultural head of these people, a man steeped in their ancient arts welcomed Wondred and his stick. He said that the stick was very special—and that he could talk with it. And yes it was perfectly true they could actually understand each other.

The stick's first communication was that his name really was 'Stick'. It kind of represented every other tree and branch, alive or dead, wherever they might be.

The Chief whose own name was Saw-saw spent some time with Stick, and conveyed the name to Wondred.

And so began a new phase in the life of Wondred and Stick. It would end in a dreadful disaster

It began, as these things often do, innocuously enough. The local council was under tremendous pressure to release more of the land under their control to develop more housing. Unfortunately they chose a large area which included the woodland which lay beside the river. As you will have guessed this was the very woodland that was so enjoyed by Wondred and Stick.

The arguments got brutal and somewhat personal. members of the council who stood to gain considerable wealth from this expansion called those against the proposal "namby—pamby do nothing twits who were burying their heads in the ground and ignoring the needs of the community." These of the "Save the trees" group complained that the others were out to make a financial killing.

And so the sides were drawn.

Stick who was obviously upset by these proceedings, took to sulking in dark corners, and when in the presence of the housing committee members he would accidentally bash his pointed end on the toes of their shoes, leaving Wondred to apologise.

But Stick could and did take positive action. That spring Stick paid many more visits to the woods than previously. And as a direct result of these visit's the trees had produced and released many times more seeds that they had hitherto. Summer came and millions of small trees began sprouting everywhere. The path became choked with new growths. It became impossible to even enter the woods.

When this was reported to the Housing Committee they funded a study as to the possible impact of this excessive growth on their plans. The report was damning. 'Even,' it said 'if the paths can be cleared, there was still the rest of the area to consider. The cost would be considerable—at least double the original estimate, and maybe more. The rate re-growth was now such as to require constant and very expensive maintenance.'

In the light of this report a number of the "build at any cost" group hatched a deadly plan. This plan was the result of sheer frustration, it was wicked, deadly, and un-professional.

They planned to set fire to the woods !!

It was the only thing that they could think of doing.

But they had to wait for a reasonable dry spell of weather and in this interval tongues would waggle and the news of their intentions eventually reached Wondred and Stick. This was now well beyond anything that Stick and Wondred could do to prevent what they considered to be a tragedy.

***

It was on a dark moonless night in mid summer at the end of several days of hot dry weather. Men with burning torches were seen struggling through the now dense growth which took the flame, made it its own and in the presence of a fairly stiff breeze became a truly massive blaze.

Unfortunately the fire moved too fast for some of the fire setters and five of their number became trapped and succumbed to the dense smoke and were consumed. Unhappily, too late Wondred realised that Stick was missing.

Wondred made for the woods. But the blaze now completely out of control and he slowly began to realise that it had taken Stick.

***

For many years a sickly smell hung over the area where trees once grew. The housing plans were scrapped. No-one wanted to live in an area where people had died terrible deaths and the area had a dismal forgotten look about it.

Wondred felt that he should move out of the area but could not bring himself to leave. Then one day, when he was very old and infirm Wondred made the trip across the river and into what was the woods. He was both surprised and pleased to see that fresh green shoots were beginning to appear.

Strangely he found one such sapling growing just where it could not be avoided. He grasped this stem and it suddenly became detached. On getting it home he found that it made a fine stick to support himself now he was no longer very steady on his feet.

He called it Stickson.

John Lord
8/8/2013

THE WHEREABOUTS

Rule 166

*Y*acob Trip; Sentinal, gathering his robe around his pathetically frail body slowly, to avoid falling, and painfully, began the long descent from The Centre to the High Terrace. He wondered, not for the first time, how many more of these occasions he would be able to manage. He was not old by the standards of the day but at fifty-three he felt the years weighing heavily on him.

Fear accompanied him as he remembered five years ago, the last time, the reaction to the words had caused something of a riot and it took the Sentinals in their grey uniforms, and carrying their weapons ready for use, to maintain calm.

He had stood there shaking and sweating unable to speak or to move for fear of turning the wrath of the crowd unto himself.

Now his mind switched to his knee and he clenched his teeth as the familiar pain penetrated it. The invidious job had to be done, failure would mean that they would simply remove him and replace him with another Sentinal.

In his shoulder bag was a tightly rolled-up document which was THE WORD.

THE WORD, Said aloud it seemed innocent enough, go on try it *THE WORD*—There you are you see nothing happened. But buried in this innocence was the future of every single individual on the surface of the globe.

He began to count '53—52—51—There were, he knew, just one hundred downwards steps to reach the platform which he was destined to stand before that pre-selected crowd and do his duty.

For him the reading of THE WORD was the culmination of a lengthy process that began with his being wakened just before dawn. He would prepare himself and eat just as Ninnima was breaking the horizon warming the place up and reaching into every corner with its brilliant pentrating beams. At the right time as indicated by the Voice he would somewhat nervously stand by the doors and enter the descender when its doors opened.

Doors smoothly slid shut and strangely he would be aware that the descender was in motion but sideways or up or down it was impossible to determine.

Doors open.

The room, if that is the correct word for it, was grandly impressive. Opulent was an understatement.

The space was so vast that the walls could not be seen, the edges in whatever direction one cared to look simply continued on until all one could see was simply a misty vagueness. Shapes could just be discerned but not identified,—perhaps imagined.

Nearer stood some dark baroque chairs and neat low tables.

Nearly all the ones that Yacob could discern were claimed by a very mixed bunch of brightly attired adult individuals. Nearly all the occupied tables carried drinks in bottles and glasses of various kinds glinting in the brilliance of the artificial lighting.

It was a strange and unsettling place.

But the procedure was natural and obvious—The centre of this space was occupied by a plain round table and a single chair. A glass with plain water was the only thing on its cold non-committal surface

It was normal procedure for the current serving Sentinal, on this occasion Yacob, to obey the gentle voice which filled his and only his ears, to please be seated.

Then after a few minutes, during which the identity of Yacob was checked and passed OK—He raised both hands high above his head to mark that the one hundred and twenty six'th People's Meeting had now begun. Then after the chattering had quietened down he announced in a voice that echoed icily around the place. Its source appearing to be unidentifiable.

He was given to say—

'The Governors ask me to say—"Welcome to the latest People's Meeting?" and they ask—"Does anyone have a question to which they need an immediate answer?"

Yacob's heart momentarily ceased to beat. It was at this point at the previous session that trouble began to move from words to actions.

A fairly bulky document appeared on the table, brought by an unseen agency.

Most of the book's contents were known to Yacob who had spent most of his life studying it.

The Book was known simply as "THE INSTRUCTION MANUAL"

The Governors question hung in the air for what seemed like half a lifetime, then—

A voice from the crowd broke the silence—

'Yes indeed—I have.'

Yacob—" *Then please identify yourself.*"

'I am known as Luke Steadly.'

"We know you Luke Steadly—What is your question?"

'The last time we met here our questions went unanswered and here we are again—our simple enquiries unattended. What do we have to do to obtain that which we would like to know?'

Yacob's heart sank—'*The statement I have from those who govern us, is that you will have that which want in due course.*'

Another, this time unidentified voice from the crowd—'That's not good enough.'

Yacob felt vulnerable—yes just where are the Government when one needs them? He tried the hard line.

'I'm afraid that is all we are permitted for now.'

A third voice—'You leave us no choice—we will have to come and find out for ourselves.'

This was just what Joseph was afraid of.

'Then let me remind you of Rule Number One-six-six.' he took the book and raised it for all to see *'It clearly states that aggressive action of any kind is not permitted, and will be prevented by all appropriate means.'* Luke answered. But he had to shout above the rising hubbub from the crowd—

'If you won't let us discuss these rules with the government we will be left with no choice but to take any actions deemed necessary to obtain the knowledge we require for ourselves.'

At this, and amid a shout of approval from the crowd, Luke drew a long knife out from under his loose cloak where it had been hidden. And before anyone could stop him—he waved it high in the air.

The result of this action was immediate and very shocking. An empty circle appeared surrounding Luke as people fought to get out of range.

Then there was a single hardly audible 'plonk' and Luke sank to the floor.

The crowd went very quiet—this was not what they had come for, and no-one knew what to do. It seemed afterwards that the whole episode had been planned and carefully practiced long ago. Men in Sentinal uniforms appeared as if from nowhere and Luke's body, he was still clutching the knife; was speedily removed. A brief inspection showed him to be quite dead.

'*This meeting is over for now,*' said Yacob, shouting to be heard above the racket which grew, '*Please return to your work or your homes. The government will advise us in due course.*'

Reaction

Such was the shock of what had taken place people were simply bewildered, wherever you looked groups would be gathered together discussing this abnormal situation.

In amongst them Sentinels could be seen out in force wandering vaguely about looking for anything out of the ordinary. Over a period of several days there grew a solid reaction which could be described by the words "Something Must Be Done". A number of separate groups appeared, their members having a set of aims broadly in common. One of these groups 'The HISTORY GROUP' was characterised by a deep feeling that the answer lay buried in their history.

'Just look for yourself—what do we actually know about our history—almost nothing. Where do we come from? It is self evident that our line does not start here on this lump of space rock. Don't you think that we aught to know? That it should be common knowledge.' Some suspected that the answer lay written in volumes of books now stored in the gigantic library called 'THE PAST'. Entry into this place was forbidden and 'guarded' by Sentinels. It remained for the exclusive use by the Governors and the only way to gain entry was by having a Pass. And Passes were not given to ordinary folk below the level of Sentinel. Applicants were closely monitored. Up until now no-one has been sufficiently interested to challenge this closed access—but it now became a priority, especially to members of The HISTORY Group.

Then there was the 'BIO GROUP' These people were puzzled by the fact that their recorded DNA did not coincide with what they knew of their relationships. They must have originated very recently, but from where?

Unfortunately there developed a rivalry between these groups which generated some humour and was considered healthy, but there was also a suspicion that gaining power for themselves was the basic motive behind group action.

In the event, it was the HISTORY GROUP that was the first to break out, and to act to find answers to their questions. Chalky (Flannel) felt that he rather than Joshua

Stack should be running the Group and promptly set about denigrating that individual at every opportunity.

But it was the HISTORY GROUP that convened a gathering of representatives from all the Groups. But before this meeting could take place a notice printed in large red letters was posted on all convenient flat places by the Sentinels. It read—

MEETING MEETING MEETING MEETING MEETING

REPRESENTATIVES FROM ALL GROUPS:
—

ARE CALLED TO A MEETING—IN THE GREAT HALL—TO REVIEW THEIR STATUS AND WHETHER THEY SHOULD BE ALLOWED TO CONTINUE OR DISBANDED IMMEDIATELY

The reaction of the Groups could have been predicted. They determined that the message behind the Notice was clearly stated in that invidious last line.

In the event no one attended the Sentinel's meeting— not a single person turned up. There grew anger amongst the Sentinels at being ignored. It was now obvious that they were (had) lost control. Control was only theirs if the rest of the people complied.

There came a pause, and it was during this pause that the HISTORY GROUP took action. This was not aggressive but nevertheless determined. They attempted to ascertain for themselves an answer to that most puzzling of questions—FROM WHERE HAD THEY EVOLVED?

***

They made a proposition to the Governors. They suggested that THE HISTORY Group identify four of their members who would be checked out by the Governors themselves. These would be then given free access to THE PAST.

Following which they would be asked to provide from their studies a short Memorandum summarising their findings.

This document would them be approved or amended and then released for general consumption.

This plan would be subject to inspection by the governors at any time, following which anything unacceptable would be removed from the document.

There would be a number of safeguards.

1. The four man team would be under the direct control of the Governors at all times.
2. No part or parts of the information gathered by the four man team shall be allowed to be available outside the workings of this team.
3. The HISTORY GROUP will accept the Memorandum as the final and only description of their history.
4. The identities of the four man team will never be made known.
5. The HISTORY GROUP will appoint two persons to review the Memorandum before general publication.

They then obtained a commitment from Sentinel Yacob to place this proposition in the Governors. 'In Tray'

In spite of Yacob's apprehension he was allowed to place the proposal in the hands of the Governors.

Nothing happened—for a while, When it did it was totally unexpected and increased the anger of the Groups to a new and very dangerous level.

The response was—That the previous notice calling for a meeting was re-issued.

***

Nothing, it appeared, that related to their history would be allowed.

Fury ranged deep and angrily in the HISTORY GROUP.

And once again NO-ONE turned up for the meeting.

Things were looking bleak.

Throughout their time, as far as was taught there had never been trouble like this. And what the Governors did not appear to understand that their denial to allow access to this very basic information was exacerbating the problem.

The Sentinels began to be ignored and minor breakings of THE RULES started to happen.

Again it was the HISTORY GROUP which was the first to openly declare its objectives. These were—

1. To agree a meeting between appointed members of the Group and the Governors.
2. The Governors will attend this meeting in person. Stand—in's will be unacceptable.
3. Questions will be made available in advance of the meeting and will be made public together with the answers following the meeting.

This request was at first rejected by the Governors, but a slew of acts of civil disobedience broke out. Such a thing had never happened before and each was more damaging than the previous one. It convinced them that the proposal had some merit. And the meeting was agreed but no date was established

It must be understood that no-one outside the Governors had ever seen any of these strange and remote individuals who were responsible for creating the document which governed them all—THE OPERATING INSTRUCTIONS.

For a moment it appeared that things were moving peacefully in the right direction until the first of the questions was issued. It was simple enough and took the form of a simple but very fundamental rule. It was—

"1. Any and all persons over the age of 15 years shall be a permitted access to THE PAST."

The Governors were quick to reply to this request with a flat refusal. The Governors were adamant that the information held in THE PAST would, if released for general consumption, be mis-interpreted and become the prime driver in the break-up of the whole of their society.

This answer caused great consternation—what was this knowledge that could so readily disrupt their way of life?

It became more important than ever to find out.

And so a few of the more forceful members of the HISTORY GROUP plotted a break in to THE PAST with the object of bringing out anything that might cause some concern. Knowledge of this leaked out and another large notice appeared—

WARNING WARNING WARNING WARNING.

ANY ATTEMPT TO ENTER 'THE PAST' WITHOUT
AN OFFICIAL PASS WILL BE SEVERELY DEALT
WITH—REMEMBER LUKE STEADLY

In truth most had forgotten Luke a loner who was not missed. But this was a reminder that he had in effect been executed, without a trial. Where was this in the INSTRUCTION MANUAL?

***

Why all this fuss about their history?

The sum total of available information in summary was sparse in the extreme.

It was ;-

1. They were a small colony of some thousand individuals.
2. They had been living together for at least two hundred years.
3. Information as to where they and when they had originated was not known.
4. As far as anyone knew it had always been this way.
5. The rules or the INSTRUCTION MANUAL had been drawn up by an unknown agency and contained all that was needed for the successful continuation of the colony. It was available only to the Governors.

6. Their history was held in the place called 'THE PAST' access to which was the privilege only of the Governors.

7. The existence of the Governors was accepted but not one had ever been seen.

8. The colony had most things needed for a comfortable life—A range of life forms which were familiar to them and pleasant scenery with sea, forests and even a mountain or two. But where were they?

9. The BIO GROUP in particular wanted to know why no children were conceived until the last 50 years, up until then all the women were barren.

10. Most of the missing information was supposed to reside in a forbidden place, access being allowed only to Sentinels

**

The Past

The people of the colony now determined that they should know something of their history. And who the Governors were. They knew that there would be a price to pay but they were at last prepared for that.

But it would be worse than they could imagine.

**

The tension in the colony was increasing as more of the people became convinced that the Governors were hiding something. And that thing was information that might disrupt the colony. More and more people recognised that the Governors were not going to allow anyone access to THE PAST. They could be destined to never know how they came to be where they were.

The HISTORY GROUP decided to break into THE PAST and a team of six of the more determined individuals took some basic tools—screwdrivers. saws. chisels, hammers and the like and set out for that place.

The Sentinels formed a small troop and failed to persuade the team to abandon their intentions but were thrust aside.

'THE PAST'—those two troublesome words were chisled into the stone lintel over the doorway which surrounded the huge metal door which, as far as anyone knew had never been opened. There was a code to open the door but it had been lost some considerable time ago.

The gang of would-be break-iners arrived at the door with their feeble tools, but felt that they had to try.

So two of their number approached the door and set to work on one of the hinges with hammer and chisel.

What happened next was to set them back and take what they were trying to do infinitely more seriously.

With the suddenness of the totally unexpected a pair of machine guns fired out from the huge door jambs riddling the two attackers of the door with bullets.

They fell where they had stood and died in a growing pool of blood.

A horrified silence followed the rattle of the guns. The rest of the troop were too stunned to move.

Back in the colony the survivors relayed the story of their dreadful experience and attempted to console the partners of the two dead men.

At the next meeting of the HISTORY GROUP feelings ran high.

The price they had already paid to gain access to something unknown was an anathema to some who were for leaving things alone.

But the majority were of the view that such an event meant that there really was something dreadfully secret inside which they had to know.

And nothing would stem the anger that this terrible incident would generate throughout the population.

They determined yet again that they must break into THE PAST and that they would find a way to achieve this.

The other effect of the attempted break in was that the Sentinels formed a small troop to prevent any further attempt. But they were ineffectual and were easily pushed aside.

***

So—in due course a grand army of volunteers was formed. The guns in the doorframe were disarmed and at last the door was opened. What they saw filled them with both amazement and apprehension.

Inside was vast and divided into sections. Each section according to its label was devoted to some aspect of humanity.

There was Human Biology, Early History, Modern History, Religion, Earth Life—forms (which was itself divided into sub sections—Amphibians, Insects, and so on). Mechanics, Mathematics, Physics, Communication, Health—and so on. All told when it was measured they found that there was eight miles of it.

The last section seemed to be the most interesting— the heading was simply

'Government'

Fortunately it was agreed that nothing should be removed.

Access to the content should be made available only inside THE PAST which was put under the management of two trustworthy individuals, and appointed a pair of Sentinels to ensure that the data was always safe.

So far—so good.

But what of the Governors?

And the INSTRUCTION MANUAL which strangely was not in THE PAST?

But there was the section labelled Government inside which was a shelf full of discs and a machine to play them on.

***

Government

This was to be the biggest shock of them all, and to leave them with a massive problem.

Who should be playing these discs and how will the information be disseminated? Who should be making these decisions?—they had no formal structure but when they asked for volunteers there were only two or three who came forward.

Old George Pantril

Ken Dull

Simon Prentiss

And Ruth Sandy got together and offered to play the discs and then to pass the essential bits by means of a News Letter in the form of Questions and answers.

The content would haunt them for the rest of their lives.

***

From the Discs—

It began with the present and the bland first statement was in itself enough to give them nightmares.

It went—

"People of 'Intruder' which is the name I SHALL USE FROM NOW ON TO REFER TO YOU.

"You have been led to believe that you are governed by a formal form of government (elected or appointed) known as the Governors. Sadly this is not the case—

"The Governors DO NOT EXIST. You have been ruled so far by specially constructed androids you know as Sentinels. The Sentinels obtain their instructions from the INSTRUCTION MANUAL the content of which is on the next set of discs.(Disk EM1-to EM1627), and which is the best distillation of all the best rules used on old planet Earth. It represents the best of human civilised management."

"History.

"Firstly you will want to know what happened to planet Earth. And simply stated

PLANET EARTH NO LONGER EXISTS.

"About fifteen hundred earth years ago a strange piece of space junk appeared to be heading for the solar system. Every attempt was made to deflect it without success.

"According to the calculations it would come close enough to Earth as to modify both trajectories. It would fling the Earth out of the solar system and the Earth would be replaced in almost the same orbit by this intruder form space. The only hope of survival from this holocaust would be to transfer from earth to the other object when they

were at their closest, thus using the newcomer as a Noah's Ark as it were.

"And so plans to do this were drawn up. If you are playing this disc then it was successful and you have millions of people on old earth who did not survive to be thankful to.

"We felt it better to tell you the story of the past slowly so as not to cause you too much upset—so the next disc will not play until at least a further two of your days has elapsed."

The effect of this information on the population could not be gauged and so it was agreed between the Groups to sit tight on it and to release it very carefully bit by bit via a specially arranged series of TV programmes over several months.

As shocking as the information was—it also explained a wide number of physical problems which hitherto had simply baffled the experts. Now they could put these effects down to differences between the old Earth and their new planet. Differences due to different levels of gravity, different mixture of gasses making up the air they breathed, A different diet provided by altered flora and fauna, and so on. The seasons were very much the same but the average day length was about 12 hours longer.

With this vast increase in knowledge a great many things began to be understood. Optimism for the future well being of the population ran high.

However—

IT WAS NOT TO BE THAT EASY

The Split

There gradually developed three different ways of thinking and thus of living.

Broadly speaking these were—

The People of Old Earth—(The POE)
These wanted to imitate all that they could find out about how the earthers lived and what they believed in.

The New Planeters.—(The NP)
Wanted to keep the place just as it was.

The New World Builders—(The NWB)
Were determined to improve their way of life.

Their aims for the future were very different. An example was what to do with the Sentinels. The POE wanted them to be dismantled since they played no part on old planet earth. The NP wanted to keep them as they were. But put them under the control of chosen members of the public. But NEB would enhance their capabilities and give them significantly more responsibility. Sadly these differences caused significant friction. In various ways the friction grew and small fights began to appear.

The supporters of each of the three polices came to be determined that their own one was the one that the whole planet should adopt. And it did not take very long for the three lots to live separate parts of the planet where they could be self governing entities. eventually skirmishes grew into fights, and fights into battles and inevitably battles into all out warfare.

The war was brutal and lasted just long enough for them to completely wipe out all they had gained, and the few that were left failed in their attempt to provide for themselves and starved to death.

Leaving a barren piece of space debris, roughly the size of the old moon, circling the old sun and carrying a small amount of decaying biological matter and the only history of the human race.

John Lord
10/10/2013

A ROYAL ISSUE

*O*ld king Optimist the Third had a problem. Not a serious problem let it be said but one that he felt badly needed resolving. And as time marched steadily onwards he felt that a solution was needed more than ever. So he decided to discuss it seriously with a number of High Officials of State. To this end he put together a list of those of whom he proposed to involve. He would of course put any conclusions before Her Majesty his wife for her (essential) approval.

So what then of the problem that was troubling his mind and interfering with his normally tranquil sleep.

Well it was one which might affect the whole of the future of the state.

It was—WHO SHOULD MARRY HIS LOVELY DAUGHTER THE PRINCESS ROYAL—ELLUISE?

Old Opty, as his intimates called him (when out of his hearing), was all too aware that his little girl had a number of followers all eager to share not only her bed but also the governing of the state. It was arguably the most powerful and influential job of them all. But could he trust any of them? And how to choose?

Firstly he needed a list of all possible suitors, and after careful consideration he elected on the following high ranking or' important' males.

1. Firstly there was Long John Maibee. Very tall, handsome and very very rich, he nevertheless had one serious draw back—he could not make a decision.

   His name told it all Maibee or should it be Maybe? Maybe it should and then again, maybe it shouldn't.

   He might be asked 'Are you going to the Fair tomorrow?'

   And the inevitable reply would be—'Er . . . maybe.'

2. Then there was William Wilkill Captain of the Guards. He had no money but oh what a manly figure he possessed—every maiden's dream. But to keep his looks he did physical jerks all day, with short breaks for meals. He was also conversationally bereft.

3. And what about Sir Monn—a cleric and an interesting person if you can interrupt his continuous and salacious monolog about the wickedness of man, and especially woman, and what they can get up to.

4. And of course one had to include C H Issel the court sculptor a man with a good clean tool, that is if his models had anything to go by.

5. One cannot ignore Bendown Forkain the royal teacher, over fond of sitting the young princes on his knee "to complete their education.". I bet he does the King thought.

6. And what about young St. Rike Wenhot the court blacksmith he could lift a cart horse with one hand and eat a sandwich with the other, but was never invited to demonstrate his prowess at this as he was likely to get mixed up and take a bite out of the animal, and fit an iron shoe to his sandwich.

7. Finally there was G. Row the gardener—good at making all manner of things come up—especially in the spring.

As a sensible king he put the list before his lady wife The Queen—Rosebud. She read the list several times, and her verdict said it all—

'Is this all there is? I wouldn't look twice at any of them. Where are the clean living and unspoilt healthy males? We need an injection of fresh blood in the family?'

The king shrugged. 'You are, I think, referring to what we call "commoners", And the royals NEVER EVER mix with them. What would happen to the royal blood if one did.' He said glumly.

'I suppose your right,' she replied. 'but please let me have some time with each before you announce the lucky chappy.' And just what she intended to do with them you may well guess.

***

Now careful observers will have noticed that one intimately involved individual has been missed out in this decision—No it's not the butler—it is the Princess herself.

When The queen, Elluise's ever loving mother, called on her the next day in order to prepare her for what the

King intended to do. Showing her the list of approvals her daughter was horrified. She had always expected to be permitted to make her own choice of partner. She was however persuaded to at least go over the list with her parents, So a formal meeting was arranged.

Each of the persons on the king's list was instructed to be on standby and to be ready to answer any questions they might be asked.

It was therefore for each a formal interview.

And it is fair to say that not one of the participants was looking forward to what was proposed.

Even Old Opti Three was worried, He was concerned that his daughter would humiliate each of the would be suitors, and choose none of them. It had taken a great deal of persuasion on his part to get them to agree to be on the list.

The suitors, each and everyone of them, were also worried—as none of them wanted to be permanently shacked up with Ellouise. She was far too demanding.

Their lives would not be their own. And all those boring Royal functions.

And especially the Queen was worried in case her daughter chose one of the ones that she herself was secretly on intimate terms with. After all the king was getting on in years and unable to bring the queen any royal satisfaction.

***

The day of the meeting duly arrived. The King was instructed to wear The Garments of State which was an enormous Leopard skin coat worn over a pair of gold shorts and which left his thin scraggy legs exposed to public view. The King was truly discomfited.

Each of the 'applicants' was attired in their best and thus their most uncomfortable clothing. Some of which reeked of mothballs.

A very nervous princess dressed to look as attractive as was possible sat between her loving parents. She and her mother were simply but elegantly attired—the queen in glorious red and her child in powder blue, a blue that rivalled the sky.

The suitors were asked to wait in the great hall to be called in, the order being determined by drawing their names out of a hat.

The first to be granted an audience was Bendown Forkain the youngest of the bunch.

He had never associated with the royal family except in a teaching capacity.

As he stood there waiting for a barage of intimate questions he had prepared himself for, he realised that the princess would probably try to get her own back and use the cane on him at every opportunity.

The thought made him feel quite queezy. He expected that she would probably enjoy it, and was suddenly shocked to find that he was also interested.

The royal interrogation began—

The Queen—'Would you continue to teach? If so could you teach me a thing or two.?'

Teach—was horrified but kept his wits.-

'I would be glad to enlighten your majesty—in any way I can.' He replied. 'Even if I fail this test'.

Before Teach could dig himself deeper into he morass of double speak. Old Opti had had enough of this smarmy individual 'OK that's enough—thank you, you may wait outside.' he said.

'Next.' It was a shout.

In strode St, Rike. He had just come from shoeing a horse and was only wearing his leather shorts.

The king heard the sharp intake of breath from her Royal Majesty and made a mental note to sack him when this was over.

'OK—Thank you.' Said the king, and caught the admiring looks from both the ladies as the blacksmith turned to leave.

The next to stand and be judged was Sir Monn, dressed for the occasion in a breast plate of silver threaded with gold—you could not look directly at him without being blinded. The King was busy assessing how much he would get for the garment from his friends in the business. He asked a question—'Where does your income come from?'

Sir Mon shuffled is feet—

'Sire the good folk of the church contribute freely each Sabbeth in exchange for a guarantee that they will finish up in heaven when they pass on.'

The King was puzzled—

'So you have the ear of GOD ?' He asked naively.

'Well—er—Not exactly.' Was the reply and they were none the wiser.

Sir Mon He knew that he had committed some grave error but he did not know what. So the man of GOD cursed under his breath and turned to leave.

C. H. Izzle the sculptor was next,. Bursting to relieve himself he opened the door of the interview room under the impression that it was the door of the male facilities.

Seeing the row of startled faces he managed to re-zip himself just in time. But not before the King had noticed. A man who could not control his flies would be too disturbing in court.

'Thank you, We will talk later in private.' Were the words of dismissal.

The Queen's favourite. The bed of magnificent flowers sited just under her window was not the only bed she shared with G Row the gardener when the rest of the royal crew were away. She risked a question. 'Did all you could to get one to come up this season?' She asked reasonably.

'Yes Maam,' Was the prompt reply, 'It was stiff and strong in the season.' He added.

And all except the King knew who was keeping Her Royal Majesty warm these cold nights.

After him there was Long John Maibe. He answered his question predictably with a shrug of his thin shoulders and a noncommittal 'Yes perhaps—I'm really not sure,' And was summarily dismissed.

And last but far from the least was Sir William Wilkill Captain of the Guards.

The King was very undecided about him, he hoped that one day this fine figure of a man would overcome his deep respect for seniority and cement a closer relationship with himself. It would make a pleasant change from the lady of his bedchamber, willing and attractive though she was. 'What are your prospects?' Asked the king knowing full well what they were.'

'Just army pay your majesty.' The good man replied.

Thank you—dismissed.' Said the King

***

And so—There you have it.

All the prospective males from the court lined up and inspected for the most important role in the land.

As the door closed after the last man. The King turned expectantly to his daughter and addressed her with his serious voice, the one he saved for declaring war.

'Well my dear did this help with your making a choice. Remember it is not only you who will have to tolerate your choice but also the rest of us and the State.

We have picked the very best for you to select from.'

'Now I am due for a holiday, two weeks fishing on England's River Tyne should set me right, and I expect you to have made your mind up by then. Say in three weeks—on December the first'.

"And Bl—dy good luck to you." he thought.

***

Whilst the King was away the participants struggled to come to terms with the thought that they might find themselves shacked up to the Royal Princess or risk the King's wroth.

And may even be ordered to do the necessary on the pain of being excommunicated or worse.

The Royal Princess was in a spin. She recognised that ultimately she would have to make a choice or have it made for her. The king would ultimately have his own way in this as he always did.

She therefore wisely decided to get to know each of the prospective citizens herself, with the help and experience of the old wizened witch and spell-binder the mistress Annie Curses.

It had to be at night (it always was in the best stories). A pale full moon occasionally hidden behind thin drifting clouds created a constantly moving scene as she picked her way along the woodland path to the woman's lair.

At last a large black cat met her on the path and walking in between her feet accompanied her to the dark wooden dwelling that was the place.

'Come in my dear, I am expecting you.' A hoarse woman's voice called out as she approached the open door.

'I have made you a drink which you must take—it will make you only tell the truth. Please sit.' She indicated a cushion and the Princess sank gratefully down on it. She was tired it was a hard path.

'You must be tired—it's a hard path.' Said Annie.

A period of quiet followed, in which only the noises of the surrounding forest could be heard. After Witch, as it were—she began—

'I do not envy your having to choose one of this gang of individuals to be your ever loving and father of your children. But if I can help I will—So what do you wish me to do?'

'Thank you, I would like your thoughts on each of them.'

'Yes, that is your right, but please bear in mind that they may react differently to me.'

'So who is to be first then?'

The princess considered for a short while—then—

'The rich Long John Maibe?'

The witch considered for a few moments then gave just one short phrase—

'He may come or he may not.'

And that was it.

'The Guards Captain William Willkil?'

A short pause, then—

'All he has is his sword, but he is good with it.'

'The good cleric Sir Monn?

'You will not be satisfied by Hymn.'

' The sculptor Mr Isle?'

'His tool will be sharp but not just for you.'

'The school master Bendown'

'He may do just that for anyone.'

'St Rike Whenhot the blacksmith?'

'He will quench your thirst with water.'

'Old Grow the gardener?'

'He will plant his seed but once a year'

There ensued a longish pause.

'Well that's the lot.' Said the princess. 'You have given me your thoughts to go away with—they will certainly be inconsiderable help. And your fee—' She handed over a bag which was heavy with gold coins.

They said there goodbyes and the crone wished the young one all the best.

Back in the palace—the princess began to realise that she was no nearer to selecting the man she was expected to spend the rest of her life with—through thick and thin, good and bad, joyful and sad, richer and poorer (not keen on the latter) she thought.

Who's daft idea was it that the heir to the throne must be capable of and want to produce offspring?

After a while and in the absence of any better ideas— the princess decided to discuss the problem with her mother the Queen.

Having decided to do this Elluise arranged a private interview with her Mother—at least that lady should be able to draw on a lifetime of experience in matters marital.

Unfortunately the King had just cut one thousand Twiggs from her Majesty's weekly allowance in order to purchase a new and very fast car for himself, and she was not best pleased. But on mature reflection and with a bit of luck he might just kill himself in it. The thought cheered her up considerably.

'Come in,' the queen sang out in response to her hesitant knock, and as Elluise entered—'And for Pete's sake do sit down—I think I can guess what this charade is all about—He's sent you to spy on me.'

'Er no, it's about me.' Said the girl, She always felt nervous in the presence of Her Majesty.

'You!,' exclaimed the Queen. 'Your only worry is to pick the richest man. And your laughing.'

'If it were that easy I wouldn't be here.' She responded. 'They each have some aspect of character that I like, but I am not in love with any of them.'

'Then pick the richest.' Was the prompt reply. For her it all seemed so easy

'That would be John Maibee, but he can't make up his mind.'

'Perfect.' Said Her Majesty. 'You can make it up for him.' And with a wave of her hand indicated that the interview was at an end.

***

Our Princess then applied for an audience with the King in order to acquaint him with her choice.

'Why him?' Asked that Royal person, 'He can never decide on anything.'

'I love him.' She lied.

And so that noble individual was advised as to his future—and was amazed. After all why him? It was a puzzle.

In due course the great day arrived—flags fluttered from every building. The church bells rang forth from sunrise to sunset, and the day was fine.

Everyone who counted and many a one who didn't was present. The Cathedral was packed.

It was all going well up to that point when the good cleric says to the prospective groom—'Will you take this person to be your lawful wedded wife to have . . . until death do part?'

John Maibee's reply was typical—

With a face screwed up with concentration he said— 'Er—Er—Er—I am really not sure.'

And that was it. It was all over.

Poor John was unable to commit with the two small words—"I Do."

The wedding was disbanded and the bill was sent to John Maibee who paid it without protest.

And now—

The king is long since passed on. Allouise is Queen and lives with her Mother in the palace as does John Maibee—well maybe he does or maybe he doesn't he still can't make up his mind.

John Lord
24/10/2013

MURDER—THE ONLY WAY

*S*he'd had enough. No I mean she had really had enough. How she had tolerated what he had dealt out to her over these ten long years since their wedding was a mystery.

It had begun shortly after their honeymoon, On his way home from work Stan had seen a neighbour leaving their house, and knowing her to be on her own at that time of day, he held a picture in his mind of the pair of them in bed. Nothing could be farther from the truth— the kind chap from next door was merely re-delivering a wrongly posted letter. This simple explanation was not believed, and to her shock he hit her across her mouth as a reminder he said 'of what would happen if he caught her "at it". The blow drew blood and she had a swollen lip for some days. What was worse was that he had never done anything like that before. But if she thought that it was an isolated incident she was about to be disillusioned.

There followed a series of warnings as he left for work in the morning. He worked the dayshift then and she learned to keep out of his way when he arrived home especially if, as was often the case, he had stopped off for a drink on his way from the firm.

Don't get me wrong—under normal pleasant circumstances he could be kindness itself and generous to a fault especially to outsiders. An engaging and fun loving personality he could become a very different person with a drink or two inside him. She remembered that second time, she was heavily pregnant when he got the idea into his head that the baby was not his. Where this came from she had no idea.

She had just got out of the bath when he appeared and punched her twice in the belly. The result was certain—she miscarried. What was worse was that the injury was such as to make further pregnancies impossible a fact for which he blamed her in spite of a good portion of the medical fraternity telling him that the blow was the cause.

If she thought that was bad enough there was more to come, much more.

She tried hard to keep out of the way of eligible male company and mostly succeeded, but it was Stan who suggested that she went out to work in 'order to bring in a little extra cash,' he said.

But she new that the real reason was to keep her from meeting other men.

It was in fact OK from that point of view as the work entailed a little light cleaning for two or three local ladies who had full time jobs and no time for housework.

There was a flaw, however, Mrs Alderbury at number twelve also had a son who was a writer, and wrote from their home.

It was, she later admitted, a mistake not to tell Stan. When he discovered that she was alone in the house with him for two or three hours—he simply went wild, accusing her of every sexual activity in the book and several not in the book.

On that occasion he succeeded in putting her in hospital. The hospital staff had of course seen it all before and the standard procedure was to put her in touch with a good counsellor. His verdict was to get out of the marriage as soon as possible before Stan killed her.

Then one day when she was at home on her own she was startled to hear the rattle of a key being turned in the front door and in walked Stan who turned round and said to someone behind him 'Come in.' And there stood Stan grinning at her whilst he was ushering in a man she had never seen before.

Stan was at his best and showing off to the newcomer.

'Meet my wife Dave, Dave this is Sherl short for Shirley, Sherl this is Dave, and we've dropped in for a cup of tea. We've earned a couple of hours off, isn't that right Dave.' It was a statement not a question.

She brought them a pot of tea and some cakes and left them in the lounge to chat whilst she busied herself in the kitchen.

'See you later darling, we have to be back for the end of the lunch break, come on Dave we don't have much time.'

And they were off.

She saw quite a lot of Dave over the next few months, always with Stan and she grew to like him. He had many little gestures such as bringing her a few flowers to thank her for her hospitality. And then there was the day when she was alone with him. Stan had gone out to get some beer. He patted her bottom in a more than merely friendly way, and she discovered that she liked it.

Sadly Stan suspected something and beat a confession out of her.

***

It turned out that Dave was an outdoor man, keen on walking the fells, and being single was often away visiting the wilder parts of Britain. Soon Stan became interested and the pair were often away mostly at weekends clambering up some peak or other.

Occasionally the three of them would make a long week end of it.

Stan did not take this situation lightly and there were many times when he lashed out at her suspecting some quite innocent action as being an overt sexual act.

Dave was sympathy itself but professed that he was unable to help her. In this charged atmosphere Shirley and Dave fell in love, or that is what they told each other.

Then one disastrous day Shirley was again hospitalised, on this occasion she was interviewed by the police as a victim of GBH. Dave came to see her nearly every day.

'Look!' He said you can't go on like this, one day he will kill you. We aught to do something about this.'

'Well what can I do?' She asked.

Dave was silent for a while and then said very quietly—

'We will have to kill him.'

Shirley thought that she must have mis-heard him

'What did you say?'

'I believe that it is either your life or his. And I would rather it were his. I mean it so don't say anything just think about it'

To say that she was shocked was an understatement, but as there was no let-up in the beatings, in fact they got worse, she came to accept that it might be the only way.

She knew that he would not accept a divorce or a separation, more beating resulted from her daring to suggest such things.

***

As with some things, their intentions went rapidly from discussions to plans. And eventually it was decided that Dave would take the opportunity when on some serious climb to send Stan to his death from a high top with a simple push. Dave would do his best for his friend having first made sure that he was dead.

He would then marry her after a sufficient period of time.

Eventually the day of the deed arrived.

Stan and Dave set off for a strenuous climb in Scotland where unknown to Stan Dave had already been to study the prospects.

'I'll soon be back to collect you.' He said to her as they left. 'So goodbye for now.'

***

And that was the last she saw of him or of her Stan.

She waited for a message all the next day—nothing.

She rang the Mountain Rescue—nothing.

She phoned the B&B they were supposed to be staying at—nothing.

She phoned the police—nothing.

She contacted all the local hospitals—nothing.

It was two long months later that she posted them missing. She even drove up to the place and asked around—nothing.

Eventually she accepted the fact that something had gone wrong with the plan and either one had killed the other and had gone into hiding probably abroad.

Shirley made up her mind to make the most of the situation. She lodged a separation, moved home, developed new friends, and began a new life.

***

It was several years later when she was on holiday in Madeira with her new husband and enjoying a splendid meal in one of the better restaurants when she got a terrible shock. There standing at the bar was Dave. He was much changed, bronzed and leaner but unmistakable.

The shock left her breathless and totally bewildered but before coherent thought returned he looked over and instantly recognition showed on his face.

He hesitated but then leaving the drinks on the bar he walked slowly over to her. She felt like running but fascination held her. Husband now forgotten.

'Well,' Dave said 'Hallo.'

Anger tore at her as she struggled to speak

'What the hell happened?' She got out finally.

He looked embarrassed, but stood his ground. His next words gave her a second shock.

'We fell in love.' He said simply . . . . 'We live together near here.'

She was speechless, as he stood there looking somewhat embarrassed.

And before she could think of an adequate reply, with sheepish grin he said—

'We're sitting over there why don't you join us—Stan will be tickled pink to see you again.'

Her reply as she rose to leave—is unprintable.

John Lord
22/10/2013